"Don't y... get lonely out here?"

Sara asked. "This is beautiful country and all, but if I were you, I'd miss people."

Adam couldn't help noticing everything about Sara. She was attractive. Appealing. Almost endearing. He would have turned away and fled if there was anywhere else to go. He finally found his voice. "I don't miss people at all."

"But you did once, didn't you?" Sara's words were soft, gently spoken. Without realizing it, she'd drawn on her internal resources to express the spiritual love Adam needed. The love that he'd banished from his wounded soul.

He stiffened. "My life is none of your concern, so don't try fixing it."

That statement acted like a bucket of ice water in Sara's face, negating the compassion blossoming in her heart. If anybody's life needed fixing, it was hers. Still, she sensed that Adam needed her in his life—more than he even realized....

VALERIE HANSEN

was thirty when she awoke to the presence of the Lord in her life and turned to Jesus. In the years that followed she worked with young children, both in church and secular environments. She also raised a family of her own and played foster mother to a wide assortment of furred and feathered critters.

Married to her high school sweetheart since age seventeen, she now lives in an old farmhouse she and her husband renovated with their own hands. She loves to hike the wooded hills behind the house and reflect on the marvelous turn her life has taken. Not only is she privileged to reside among the loving, accepting folks in the breathtakingly beautiful Ozark Mountains of Arkansas, she also gets to share her personal faith by telling the stories of her heart for Steeple Hill's Love Inspired line.

Life doesn't get much better than that!

The Wedding Arbor
Valerie Hansen

Love Inspired

Published by Steeple Hill Books™

STEEPLE HILL BOOKS

Steeple
Hill™

ISBN 0-373-87084-1

THE WEDDING ARBOR

Copyright © 1999 by Valerie Whisenand

Visit us at www.steeplehill.com

Printed in U.S.A.

Call unto me and I will answer you and
will tell you great and hidden things
which you have not known.

—*Jeremiah* 33:3

To my special prayer partners, Angie, Bette, Brenda, Chris, Karen, Wanda and the wonderful, caring ladies of the Seekers Sunday school class.

Chapter One

"How do I get myself into these things?" Sara Stone said to herself, gripping the steering wheel of the compact car and hoping the road ahead hadn't washed out. Not that she'd know for sure until it was too late!

Peering into the sheeting gray rain she gritted her teeth and pressed on. Red-clay-colored runoff water was cresting uneven berms on the upper side of the road, carrying with it rocks the size of tennis balls and all sorts of other rubble.

Sara's knuckles were white on the wheel. She started to pray silently for safety, then paused, uneasy. There was a time when she had blithely sworn God answered all her prayers. Lately, however, she found herself anything but confident.

"Please, Lord?" she said cynically, only half believing she'd be heard. "I'm nowhere near ready to die. Okay?"

Suddenly the compact little hatchback began to fishtail. Losing traction it kept sliding no matter what she did. Finally it came to rest precariously on the edge of the roadway. One rear wheel hung off in space. The other was bumper-deep in the sticky clay.

"I can still get out of this." She gunned the motor. The wheels spun. The car's chassis shuddered and bucked as it sank even deeper into the mire.

Disgusted, Sara shut off the engine, sat back and took a deep breath. Rumbles of thunder shook the skies. Isolated and alone, she held perfectly still, waiting for whatever peril was sure to follow. Her whirling mind returned again and again to the old comedy line about being in "a fine mess."

If only she hadn't panicked and run away when the police refused to believe she was being stalked. Tensing, she glanced in the direction she'd come, half expecting to see the headlights of Eric's car. That would serve her right, wouldn't it?

Samson's ears pricked up. He raised his broad, white head to stare at the door, then at his master, Adam Callahan.

"You should have thought of that before the rain started," Adam warned gently. "If I let you out now you'll have to spend the night on the porch."

The enormous white dog looked back at him wisely.

"I mean it, boy. There's no room in this cabin for a soggy dog the size of a Shetland pony. I don't care how lovable you are."

Samson rose. Walking slowly to the door he appeared to listen for a moment before returning to stand beside Adam's chair. His chin rested on the man's knees, his chocolate-brown eyes pledged sincerity. When Adam made no move, the dog nudged him gently.

"Okay, but you won't like it out there. You're going to get soaked."

Already waiting at the door, Samson was not wagging his tail, an unusual reaction Adam found rather disquieting. "Don't go far." He flicked on the porch light and eased open the door.

The dog burst out into the night. Adam's jaw dropped. "Hey, you, come back here!"

Adam pulled on a yellow slicker with a hood, and heavy, black rubber boots. Quickly snapping them he stepped out onto the porch to peer into the storm. Samson's distant baying was the only clue to where he'd headed.

Adam left the cabin at a trot. The next time that mangy ball of fur wanted to go out in the rain he was going to tie a long rope to his collar and stand on the porch holding the opposite end.

"My next house is going to have a spare room to

keep wet dogs in,'' he murmured, starting into the forest. ''And my next dog is going to be a miniature dachshund, or some other little breed, instead of a Great Pyrenees. It'll have short hair and stubby legs. Then let's see it get away from me in the middle of an Arkansas monsoon!''

Sara hadn't moved from the driver's seat since she'd lost control of the car. She had no idea whether it was safe to climb out.

Making a droll face she remembered praying for patience and wondered what kind of sense of humor God must have. If there was a God, after all.

She recalled her recent disillusionment with Eric Rydell. He'd been hired to teach sixth grade in the school where she taught kindergarten and first. She had trusted him implicitly and introduced him to all her friends. She'd even taken him to church with her until she'd discovered what an accomplished liar he was. His pious, conventional facade was so convincing that most of her acquaintances still refused to believe how unstable he was. They were trying to talk her into getting back together with him! What she really needed was their moral support.

In truth, it was the man's unnatural possessiveness that most frightened her. None of her fervent prayers for deliverance from it had been answered. She swore he had even begun watching her house. That was when she'd taken matters into her own hands, rented a different car in which to make her escape, and headed for the Ozarks. Maybe, by the time school started again in the fall, he'd have gotten over his ridiculous obsession with her.

And maybe not. Her heart sped, her palms sweating. Had she imagined getting a glimpse of his car in her rearview mirror back on the highway? Were his threats genuine? And if so, had he noticed when she'd turned off the paved road? Or was she simply conjuring up demons where there were none?

The storm raged on. A bolt of lightning struck. Sara flinched and felt the car shift slightly. Tiny hairs prickled at the back of her neck and her forearms. The car offered more protection than she'd find outside in the wilds but there was something immensely disquieting about teetering on the edge of goodness-knows-what while she waited to slide into oblivion!

Sara jerked open the driver's side door before she could change her mind. She felt the car's precarious balance change. The roar of a rain-swollen river echoed from somewhere behind. It sounded so close. That ended her choices. No way was she going to take the chance of sliding into the water, car and all!

"Okay, okay," she told herself. "Take it easy. The main thing is, to not panic."

She eased her left leg out and placed one foot on the ground. Reaching for the waterproof backpack containing personal items and her precious laptop computer, she eased it past her chest and out into the rain as she stood up.

"Oh, yuck!" Mud squashed beneath and all around her sandals. It oozed between her toes. Wind-driven rain plastered her clothing to her body like panty hose sticking to bare legs on a humid, southern summer day.

"There are no bears, there are no bears," Sara chanted. "There are no...*aaah!*"

She clutched the pack to her chest like a shield. The fingers of one hand covered her lips to stifle a squeal. A dingy-white specter rushed out of the underbrush and headed straight for her.

Sara tried to half fend it off, half catch it. She screamed, her high pitch carrying well above the din of the storm.

The animal's greater weight and momentum propelled them both backward into the mud. She was quite relieved to realize it was a dog and not a deer or a mountain lion. It stood above her and slobbered friendly greetings all over her face and neck. Sara tried in vain to sit up.

"Get off me, you big ox. Now!"

"Just tell him to get down," a male voice quickly offered.

"He *is* down. We both are. Oh, my..." Her last statement ended in a gurgled shriek as the dog renewed its efforts to lick her face with a tongue as wide as her palm.

Twisting her head she blinked hard against the rain and tried to get a better look at the stranger.

"Are you okay?" The man's voice was gruff.

"Oh, fine. Just peachy." Sara continued to try to forcibly remove the determined animal. "Would you mind?"

"Samson." The enigmatic stranger spoke with authority. "Down. Let the nice lady go."

After one parting swipe with his tongue the dog backed off. Sara felt imbedded in the soggy ground and pushed herself into a sitting position, trying to avoid getting any more mud on the precious pack.

Looking up, she tossed her head to swing her bangs out of her eyes, then reached up to smooth the blond hair back with one hand. She realized too late that she had just drawn a band of red clay across her forehead.

"That was cute." The man was not smiling.

"I'm so glad you're impressed." Sara was anything but amused, herself.

"Actually, I'm not," the blue-eyed man said. "I can understand my dog wanting to come out in the rain, but I'd think a person like you would have more common sense."

"I was trying to find my great-grandmother's old homestead."

"In the middle of this storm?" His tone said more about his opinion of her poor planning than his actual words.

"It wasn't raining when I left home."

"So, why didn't you turn around when you saw what the weather was like?"

Sara was not about to admit she'd been running away. "I couldn't turn back. The road was too narrow. The visibility was bad."

He snorted with derision. "You mean, you might have wound up in a ditch if you'd tried to go back? Seems to me that's exactly what did happen."

"It wasn't my fault. I slid backward." She was growing exasperated with his know-it-all attitude. Wiping one hand on her ruined skirt she held it out to her would-be rescuer. He made no move to help lift her the rest of the way. She stared up at him. "Well?"

"Well, what?"

"Well, aren't you going to give me a hand?" She hoped he didn't remember that stale old joke and literally applaud her predicament.

"You said you're not hurt. I'm glad. The way I see it, you got here all by yourself—in spite of the worst storm we've had this season—so you must be the independent type. Why should you need me for anything?"

Sara struggled to her feet to face the man eye to eye. She was disappointed to find she'd have had to stand on a box to avoid literally looking up to him. Clearly, she needed to do something to alleviate his annoyance. Perhaps if she introduced herself...

"I'm Sara Stone." She shielded her face from the downpour with both hands and tried to smile. "Who are you?" For a few uneasy moments she thought he might refuse to tell her.

"Adam Callahan," he finally said.

"I could use some help with my car, Adam. Please?"

He glanced past her shoulder to eye the stranded vehicle with disdain. "Do I look like I have a tow truck?"

That did it. Sara was through trying to be polite. She was drenched and freezing. There was a fair chance Eric would drive up and accost her at any moment. And the new laptop computer she had finally decided to buy was likely to be ruined if she didn't get back in the car soon.

"If you could just help me push the stupid car, I'll gladly go away." She had to shout to be heard above the noise of wind and rain.

"It's much too dangerous to drive anywhere while the roads and creeks are flooded."

She made a disgusted face. "So, what do you recommend I do?" Noting the perplexity in Adam's expression she couldn't help grinning. "Besides, take a flying leap, I mean."

He glanced over at the muddy, blue hatchback. "Looks to me like you almost did that, already."

"I know." Wide-eyed, she suddenly realized how close she had come to sliding into the rain-swollen gully. "I've never driven on anything but smooth pavement before."

"I don't doubt that."

Sara watched him study the car's hazardous position. "Can we push it?"

"Sure." He shot her a cynical look. "You put your water wings on, get behind it, and push while I steer."

"Very funny." She faced him with her hands on her hips, keeping her stance wide for better balance due to the rising wind. She sure wished she'd worn something more suitable for stomping around in mud and water.

Adam turned away, ignoring her. He scanned the nearby underbrush, then broke a long, bare limb off a fallen tree. Swinging it around he gave Sara a momentary start until he placed it under the stuck rear bumper of her car and got into position to lift with his shoulder.

"You go over to the other side. Open that door so you can get a good hold and push from there," he ordered.

"My camping gear will get rained on."

"If it isn't waterproof you got cheated when you bought it. Do you want my help, or not?"

"I do, I do." She pressed her hands and inside shoulder to the door frame. "Okay. Ready when you are."

"Now!" he shouted.

Sara held her breath and strained with all her might.

The tree limb snapped with a loud crack. Adam yelled and his hood fell back. Sara jumped away. She could finally see the dark, thick hair and chiseled features he'd had hidden beneath the yellow slicker. She could also see he'd given up his attempt to help.

"It's no use," he shouted. "We can't do it by hand."

"Okay. Now what?"

"How should I know? If I had a brain in my head I'd leave you here and go home where it's warm and dry. But I can't do that, can I?"

For the first time since they had met, Sara thought beyond the immediate present. If Adam wasn't going to leave her, then he must intend to keep her with him. That presented a whole new set of problems. Was it safe to go anywhere with a man she'd known for only a few minutes? Could she trust him?

"Go ahead. Leave me here." Sara put on a brave front. "I'll just wait till the storm passes."

"And then what? In case you haven't noticed, that old wreck of yours is axle-deep in mud."

"Don't worry about me. I'll be fine. I have a sleeping bag and plenty of provisions."

"Where?"

"In the back seat and under the hatchback."

"How do you propose to reach them without falling off the cliff?"

"Well, I..."

Adam scowled at her. "I thought so. I suppose you'd better come with me then. My conscience won't let me leave you here. Come on. I'll take you to my place."

Sara didn't move. She insisted she wasn't afraid. Not really. She just couldn't make up her mind whether or not it was a good idea to go with him. The safest choice was to continue to decline his neighborly offer, no matter how innocent it was.

He wiped his wet face with a quick pass of one strong hand and pushed his hair off his forehead. "Well?"

"I'm not going with you."

"Fine. In that case, I think you should know one thing. These hills are riddled with limestone caves. Every once in a while, when the soil gets water-logged like it is now, the ceiling of one of the caves collapses."

"I don't believe you."

Adam eyed the contents of her car. "Have you got a tour book in there?"

"Yes. Why?"

"Look it up. There's a big one in southern Missouri. Grand Gulf, I think they call it. A cave roof fell in and created such an impressive canyon they made a state park out of it."

Sara had been analyzing him as he spoke, trying to accurately judge his truthfulness. After being fooled so completely by Eric, she no longer trusted her intuition. Still... "You're not kidding, are you?"

"Nope." He held out his hand. "Well?"

She hesitated, changing her mind repeatedly. Should she? Shouldn't she? The idea of being warm and dry certainly sounded appealing, even if she was forced to listen to more of the man's unwarranted criticism while in his company.

Adam shook his head in disgust as another bolt of lightning struck across the wooded valley. "That was too close. I'm not going to stand here and beg while we both freeze to death or become toast." He reached down and grabbed her wrist.

Sara gasped. "Hey! What...?"

"I'm taking you home with me, lady, and if you scream or pitch a fit I'm going to let go and leave you right here. I'll be happy to forget my idiotic dog ever led me to you. Got that?"

"Perfectly." She made a successful grab for the strap of her pack, lurching and stumbling along behind Adam.

The man had a valid point. It was pretty stupid to just stand there and argue. When he'd had time to calm down she'd tell him exactly what she thought of his high-handed tactics.

But I'll do it politely, if it's still raining, she added, shivering. Being warm and dry sounded wonderful. She wasn't about to risk being pitched out into the storm again because she was too outspoken.

Chapter Two

"Watching history on television does *not* prepare a person for this," Sara shouted. "How in the world did the women cope in long skirts back then?"

"They probably didn't go brush-busting in the first place." He lifted her feet off the ground as he pulled her up behind him on a rocky ledge. "We aren't taking the usual trail. It's too far that way. The sooner I get out of this blasted weather the better I'll like it."

"How much farther is it?" She was breathless.

"Just up this hill and through the little valley beyond."

Sara didn't want him to let go of her wrist because she was afraid she might not be able to keep up without help. The ground beneath her ruined sandals was slippery. She'd lost her footing repeatedly.

She'd barked her shins and torn her skirt on brambles and briars. Not to mention almost winding up impaled by a deadly-looking tree with thousands of three-inch-long thorns!

"What happened to your dog?" she asked.

"Knowing Samson, he's bringing up the rear to make sure we both get home okay."

"Good. I'd hate to have anything bad happen to an animal that likes me so much."

Adam gave a hard tug and pulled her up beside him. They were balanced on a narrow rock ledge beneath the canopy of a gigantic oak. The leaves didn't stop all the rain but they did offer a slight respite from the wind-driven torrent.

"Yeah. I don't understand that," he said, scowling. "He's supposed to treat his family like a flock of sheep and be really leery of outsiders."

"Guess he could tell I was friendly." Sara looked up into her companion's deep-blue eyes and wondered for an unguarded instant if she was crazy to have placed all her trust in the rugged-looking, taciturn stranger.

Sensing her uneasiness, Adam softened his expression. "Look, lady. I promise I won't hurt you. I really am trying to keep you out of danger and get us both back inside before we catch pneumonia."

"I know." She gave him a sweet, trusting smile. "If I had to get stuck anywhere, I'm glad it was on your road."

His approachable countenance faded. His eyes darkened to the color of the foreboding sky. "I wish I could agree with you."

Sara wasn't sure exactly what kind of home she had expected Adam's to be. Certainly not anything as tiny as the cabin to which he led her.

The house sat at the edge of an apparently large clearing. The farthest perimeters were obscured by continuing rain. Square and made of stacked logs, his home looked like something straight out of a history book. Except for electric lighting and, she fervently hoped, indoor plumbing.

Adam led the way onto the porch, shook himself free of his slicker and stamped the loose mud off his boots. He turned to look down at Sara as if just now realizing who and what he had dragged home.

"Looks cozy." She managed a fairly convincing smile even though her teeth were chattering.

"It is—for one person." He paused at the door.

Sara understood his reluctance to invite her in, given her disgusting, filthy condition. "Is there any way I can get the mud washed off my back before we go inside? I don't want to dirty your nice cabin."

Adam's expression was cynical. "I'm a bachelor. What makes you think the house is any cleaner than *you* are?"

"Well, I…" She knew she was blushing but there was no way to stop. In spite of the man's contentious attitudes and mercurial moods she kind of liked him. Which meant that his teasing affected her more than it normally would have.

He took her by the shoulders and turned her around, checking the parts of her clothing she could only assume were as ghastly as they felt.

"You'll do," Adam said. "Rain washed the worst of it off. By the time we both get clean and dry the place will be a mess, anyway. Come on." He opened the door and ushered her inside, giving her a cautious but firm shove between the shoulder blades.

Sara felt Samson try to scoot through the door beside her. Only Adam's presence of mind and stern command kept the sopping-wet dog from joining them. "No. Out!"

"Can't he come in, too?"

"You and I will dry him off later. After we get ourselves taken care of." Adam paused and frowned. "That is, providing I can come up with enough towels."

Hugging her pack to her chest, Sara scanned the narrow, rectangular room. The place looked more like a hunting or fishing lodge than it did a house. There was a half-full dog dish the size of grandma's Dutch oven tucked beside a long-legged, antique gas stove in the kitchen area. Next to the food sat a water bowl nearly as big.

The remainder of the room seemed to be centered

around a coal-black, wood-burning behemoth. It sat on abbreviated legs, silently radiating heat and looking just like a pudgy oil drum with cast-ron decorations.

Sara hesitated. The place smelled very masculine. Oh, not like old socks or anything. Just different. As if a man, *this* man, had made it his private den. Clearly, the cabin was his special sanctuary. And she was an intruder.

"Really, I..." Embarrassed, Sara hung back close to the door. She didn't want to impose any more than she already had. Yet what choice was there? All her camping gear and clothing, except what she carried in the one small pack, was back at the car, inaccessible. If she were in her companion's shoes she would gladly offer shelter and assistance, so why did it bother her so much to accept the same from him?

Adam had removed his boots and was stoking the wood stove, oblivious to her uneasiness. "Slip off your shoes and leave them on the rug there by the door." He flipped open the cast iron door with a noisy clank and poked the dying embers with a stick. "I'll take care of them later."

Sara suddenly felt his gaze settle on her, warming her far more than the stove. She tensed. "What? What is it? Did I do something wrong?"

Grumbling, Adam looked away. "No. Just hurry up, will you? I'd like to get out of my wet clothes."

Her eyes widened. "Excuse me?"

"There's only one bathroom. I don't intend for us to share it, okay?" He gestured with a tilt of his head. "Over there. Through that door. And don't use up all the hot water."

Sara giggled softly. "The bathroom is *inside*, isn't it? I mean, you're not going to tell me I have to walk across the yard and back?"

"Don't be ridiculous. Of course it's inside." One corner of his mouth lifted in a lopsided smile, then quickly resumed its usual moody position. "I have a generator for the electricity to pump the water, too, so you won't have to go fetch it from the well in a bucket."

"Oh, good."

"I thought you'd appreciate that." The wry smile threatened to reappear. "There are towels in the cabinet under the sink, I think. If not, that means I didn't remember to do the laundry and we're both up the creek."

"Please," Sara said, "don't mention creeks or rivers or anything else pertaining to water. I don't think I've ever been this wet."

"Stick around these hills long enough and you'll get used to it," he told her. "Locals say, if you don't like the weather, just wait a few minutes and it'll change. It's kind of a standing joke."

"I can believe that." She was eyeing the bathroom door. "Um, I do have one other request, if you don't mind."

"What is that?"

"Well, there's a sweatshirt and some personal things in my pack but I don't have any other dry clothes with me at the moment. Do you suppose you could loan me something to wear? Just till my skirt dries."

"Yeah, sure. I think I can find something that will fit you."

To Sara's surprise he went to the bed instead of the dresser and dragged a low, flat, storage box from beneath it. Straightening, he tossed a pair of jeans her way as if they were of no consequence, but she could tell by the expression on his face that he cared very much about whoever the clothing belonged to. Or *had* belonged to.

Was he was hiding out up here in the wilderness to lick his wounds? Recovering from a disappointing love affair? Well, why not? She was.

"Thanks," Sara called back, as she headed for the bathroom and ducked inside. The room was spartan but definitely adequate. Turning on the shower she quickly shed her ruined clothes and stepped into the spray. Oh, it felt good to be clean!

Reveling in the warmth she let her mind wander where it wanted. Life was so confusing. Sometimes, it seemed as if she were stumbling along without purpose or guidance. At other times, like now, it was as if God had taken an interest in her future, after all.

She sighed. If that were so, there would be no real accidents in her life, would there? Not even slippery roads and unbelievable thunder storms.

Not even meeting Adam Callahan.

Adam sat on an upended log beside the wood stove and stared at the bathroom door. How long had it been since anyone else had been in his house? It seemed like forever.

He vividly recalled Gene's last visit. They'd had a great time getting reacquainted. Older by ten years, Adam had always felt responsible for his brother's welfare, even after they'd both grown up and gone separate ways.

Adam had even offered to quit the force so they could go into business together. Gene had insisted he had his own plans. Plans that didn't include settling down to a regular nine-to-five job. He wanted to have fun. Explore the wild side of life. If he hadn't had a cop for a brother, he might have succeeded.

Blinking away the final scene in his brother's short life, Adam got to his feet. It should have been him who died, not Gene. Adam was the unlucky one. The jinx. It wasn't safe to be around him. Which was one of the reasons he always gave for his life of isolation.

His thoughts returned to his guest. Sara Stone was spunky. Most women in her shoes would have collapsed in tears. She was definitely not his type, though. Which was for the best. The last thing he needed or wanted was to become involved in someone else's personal life.

As if on cue, Sara called out from behind the bathroom door. "Excuse me?"

"Yes?" he replied.

"I hate to bother you, but I just unwrapped my sweatshirt and it's damp. Got one I can borrow till it dries?"

"Sure. Hang on." He found a gray fleece that would do. "Here."

The slim, smooth arm she held out from behind the almost closed bathroom door gave him a start. She had long, tapering, expressive fingers, and delicate, unblemished skin that looked softer than satin.

Adam slapped the rumpled sweatshirt into her hand and turned away. What was the matter with him? Had he been alone so long that any woman, even Sara Stone, looked good to him?

What's wrong with the way she looks? he admonished himself, analyzing his curious thoughts. What difference did it make? He didn't intend to relinquish his hard-won tranquility for any reason. All he wanted was to be left alone. Period. End of story.

Reaffirmed, he hunkered down by the fire to wait

his turn in the bathroom. He was fine. Content. He had his dog and the wilderness, enough to eat, and a roof over his head. Plus, he could always check on the status of his investments or draw more cash by merely driving to the mom-and-pop grocery store a few miles away and making some phone calls. It was a perfect system. A perfect life.

The bathroom door slowly creaked open. Steam bearing pleasant, feminine fragrances accompanied Sara into the room. Adam found it suddenly difficult to breathe. She'd wrapped one of his towels around her wet hair and twisted it on top of her head. Her long, graceful neck arched above the loose neckline of his sweatshirt. Wisps of light, golden hair had escaped the confines of the towel to curl gently downward and caress her pale skin. Her feet were bare. And she was still lugging that ridiculous pack.

His gaze traveled Sara's full length and back to her face where she greeted him with the warmest smile and the most appealing hazel eyes he'd ever seen. This beauty was under all that mud? Heaven help him when her hair dried!

"The waist is kind of big but the jeans fit pretty well," Sara said. "Thanks." She shook out the fleecy red shirt she'd had wrapped around her laptop computer. "This isn't nearly as wet as the rest of my clothes. It should dry by the fire in no time."

"Good." Adam swallowed hard. Having her staying there, even for one night, was going to be a lot harder on him than he'd imagined. "Are you through in the bathroom?"

"For now." Sara padded across the floor to stand beside the warm stove. "I left my other clothes on the floor in the corner. As soon as you've had your shower I'll clean up everything. Okay?"

"Sure." He hoped his consternation didn't show.

"I kept my shower short so you'd have plenty of hot water."

"Thanks." Adam disappeared into the bathroom. What in the world was the matter with him? Why was he so uptight? Anybody would think he'd never been alone with a pretty young woman before.

Stripping off his shirt and jeans he threw them forcefully to the floor. *Pretty* was an understatement. How could he have been so wrong about Sara's looks? And how in the world could she have managed to smell so good when all he had on hand was his usual generic shampoo?

A quick glance at the shelf in the shower answered his question. She'd packed for any emergency, the way women did, and brought along all sorts of potions. The bottles were lined up on the lip of his shower stall like little tin soldiers.

Adam closed his eyes and stepped under the stinging spray. He placed both hands on the wall of the shower and bowed his head, letting the water cascade over him. This was the feeling he'd dreaded; the moment he'd tried with all his might to postpone. For the first time in nearly two years he was forced to admit that maybe he didn't really want to spend the rest of his life alone, after all.

Sara heard her host turn off the shower. She had hung the red sweatshirt next to the stove to finish drying and was carefully checking the condition of her portable computer. It seemed to be functioning well.

"You still there?" he called from behind the closed door.

Sara thought the question totally absurd. "Nope. I went out for pizza. Why?"

"Can't you give a simple, straight answer?"

Approaching the door she laughed lightly. "Apparently not. Is that all you wanted to ask?" She heard unintelligible muttering.

"No. I wasn't thinking. I came in here without clean clothes. Would you please hand me some?"

"Sure." Sara stifled another laugh. "Boy, with a memory like yours it's a good thing you weren't going to the store or something, huh?"

"Very funny. Just hand me a pair of jeans and a shirt. There's a stack of clothes piled on the chest at the foot of the bed."

"Okay." Complying, she noticed that nothing was folded. Not that it surprised her. She supposed a bachelor did well to just wash and dry the dirty stuff once in a while. Never mind put it neatly away.

"How shall I get them to you, shove them through the keyhole?" Sara waited for him to open the door.

Again, she overheard muttering. The poor man must really be used to his solitude. Still, even a certified grump needed a little humor in his life. And besides, she was so thankful to have been rescued she was feeling the need to share her elation.

A damp, hairy arm emerged from behind the door, fingers grasping impatiently. "Well?"

"Here." She crammed the clothes into his hand in a wad. When he didn't express any thanks she added, "You're quite welcome, Mr. Callahan."

Adam flung open the door seconds later, catching her by surprise. This was the first time she'd taken a really good look at her reluctant benefactor. He was tall and muscular. Adam Callahan was clearly a man who used his muscles. Oh, boy, was he!

Stop that! Sara lectured herself. Since when have you been nuts about grouchy Neanderthals?

"I'm not nuts." She realized belatedly that she had spoken aloud.

"Glad to hear it. Now, if you'll step out of the way I'll go tend to Samson."

"Oh, sorry." In moments she had recovered her lucidity. "Can I help? I feel like I owe it to him. After all, he did rescue me."

One of Adam's dark eyebrows raised. His deep-blue eyes peered down at her. "*Who* rescued you?"

"Well, you did, in the end. But if Samson hadn't heard my car and gone looking for me in the first place, none of this would have happened."

"Don't remind me," Adam grumbled, "or I may leave him out on the porch for the rest of his miserable life."

That stern warning sounded far too genuine. Sara placed both hands on her hips, her expression defiant. "Now look, mister. I don't want to be the cause of any trouble for that poor, innocent animal, so knock off the threats. Samson didn't do anything wrong and you know it."

"Well, well, you do have a serious side, after all, don't you? I was beginning to wonder."

"I can't help finding humor in lots of different things. It's just my nature. I guess that's one of the reasons I'm good at my job."

"Which is?" Adam grabbed a couple of large bath towels from the laundry pile and started for the door.

"I teach kindergarten and first grade."

He paused and glanced over his shoulder. "What?"

"Kids. You know, those cute, short people who like to play in the sand and eat cookies?" She chuckled at the droll expression on his face.

"I have heard of them, yes."

"I love children." She smiled sweetly, recalling the students she had just passed on to second grade.

If it hadn't been for Eric's unnatural obsession with her, she'd probably have volunteered to teach summer school. The disappointing recollection wrinkled her brow.

"So, do you have kids of your own?" Adam asked.

She sighed. "No. I'm not married."

"That doesn't seem to stop a lot of women these days."

"I'm a Christian. I have different rules of behavior. At least I'm supposed to."

"Ah." Adam nodded. "I used to be one, too."

"Used to be?"

"Yeah."

Sara could sense how uncomfortable he was so she changed the subject. "So, what do you do up here? Live off the land?"

"In a manner of speaking. Why? Do you disapprove?"

"Of course not. I'm sure lots of people do it."

"I get by."

She smiled sincerely. "Good. Which reminds me. I have a whole box of freeze-dried meals in my car. If you're short on food, I'll be glad to share mine."

"No need. There's a fresh-stewed owl in the refrigerator. We'll have plenty for supper."

Speechless, Sara gasped.

Adam's mouth began to twitch at the corners. "You should see the look on your face!"

"We're not having owl?" She swallowed hard.

"No. We're having chicken. I take it you're not opposed to eating dinner with Samson and me."

"Not a bit. As a matter of fact, I was in such a hurry to get to the Leatherwoods I didn't stop to eat. I'm starving."

"Then let's hurry up and dry the dog so we can let him in and get to the food."

"It really will be a normal meal, won't it?" she asked, hoping for further confirmation that he had been kidding.

"As normal as you'd find in any big city. I never serve ants or grubs when I have company." He was working to stifle a chuckle. "And possum is way too greasy. Too much cholesterol."

"Oh, good. Then I suppose skunk is out, too?"

"Uh-huh. Samson isn't partial to it, although he does get a kick out of chasing the little black-and-white stinkers. Tries to herd them like sheep, sometimes."

Adam opened the door to admit his soggy dog. He caught hold of the animal's ruff as it tried to push past him and quickly draped a towel over its back.

Sara grabbed another towel and followed his lead. She was almost in time to ward off a shower as the dog gave a mighty shake. "Eesh! He's a mess, isn't he?"

"Not as big a mess as *you* were when we found you."

"Which reminds me, thanks for the great rescue." Her voice took on a lilting, childish quality. "You were wonderful."

Adam was about to offer a modest response when he realized she was talking to his dog.

Chapter Three

"So, what brings you to the Ozarks?" Adam asked later, over dinner.

Sara didn't intend to admit she was running away from anything. "Oh, just a whim." Which was at least partially true.

"But why come up here? You mentioned the Leatherwoods, before. You do realize that forest has been gone for almost a century, don't you?"

"So my granny told me. It's a shame. I would have loved to see a tree with bark so strong a person could actually make shoes out of it."

"That's the way the story goes. It's my guess the finished product wasn't anything like what you and I would consider decent shoes."

She glanced at her mud-stained sandals by the door. "Well, maybe. Right now I'd settle, though."

"Don't worry. They'll dry."

Sara rubbed her arms through the fleecy sleeves of the borrowed sweatshirt. "I know." She shivered. "Do you mind if I go stand by the stove where it's a little warmer? I'm still chilly."

"Not at all. Are you done eating? There's plenty of chicken left if you want more."

"No, thanks. I'm stuffed."

"Okay. Go get warm. I'll clean up the dishes."

Sara made a silly face at him. "What did you say?"

"Go get warm."

"No, the rest of it," she drawled. "I could have sworn you mentioned doing the dishes."

"So?"

She giggled. "So, you're going to have to bribe me not to tell anybody that I actually found a good-looking guy who can not only cook, but cleans up after himself."

"I'd just as soon you didn't mention meeting me at all." His scowl confirmed how serious he was.

"Don't worry," Sara assured him. "Nobody would believe it, anyway. Far-fetched news like that falls into the same category as a sighting of Sasquatch." She smiled. "Hey! Maybe I could sell your picture to the tabloids and retire for life on the proceeds."

"I wouldn't bet on it." His voice was gruff, emotionally charged. "They didn't pay me anything the last time."

Hesitating, Sara tried to decide if he was kidding. Studying his closed expression didn't help. She quit speculating and asked. "Are you serious?"

"It doesn't matter."

"It does to me. I have a history of making rotten choices in men. I'd like to know if I'm stuck out here in the woods with a famous criminal or something."

Adam had been noticing how she glanced at the door and tensed up every time there was a crack of thunder or the wind blew debris against the windows. For the first time since they'd met, it occurred to him she might be frightened of something other than the storm.

He held up his hands for assurance, palms facing her. "I'm as honest and normal as anybody. A regular guy. Real apple pie."

Sara made a face.

"What do I have to do, stand at attention, salute and sing the national anthem to prove it to you?"

Her eyes followed the path of his gaze. A guitar was propped in a far corner. "Do you really play and sing?"

"Some."

"Oh, would you? I love folk music!" Given the natural ambience of the cabin, a wood stove for warmth, the cadence of the rain against the roof, she couldn't think of anything she'd like better than hearing a softly strummed guitar.

"Maybe all I know is rock." Adam watched her face to see what secrets her guileless features might betray. He usually played only for himself. The songs were more than company. They were catharsis. Did he really want to share that private part of his life with a stranger? He sighed. Maybe he should. If she was truly fearful, the distraction might help. The last thing he needed was to be trapped in a one-room cabin with a terrified woman.

"Anything will be fine." Sara wanted to be agreeable, above all. "Afterward, I'll help you clean the dishes."

"That's hardly scale wages for a musician."

"Maybe not, but it is a big sacrifice for me," she said. "I have an automatic dishwasher at home. All I have to do is load it. It does the whole job all by itself, even most of the pots and pans, providing I don't burn them cooking."

Adam was amused by a droll thought. He lifted the guitar carefully. "Actually, it's Samson who usually does my dishes for me. I just set them on the floor and..." The distressed look on Sara's face made him laugh. It was diverting to have such a gullible audience.

"You don't!"

"No, I don't. Except on possum night," he jibed.

"The extra grease in his diet is good for his coat. Makes it *real* shiny."

"Oh, stop!" Laughing with him, Sara made a mock swipe with her hand as he passed.

"Has anyone ever told you you're very naive?" Adam took a seat on the sofa and propped the guitar across his lap.

"I'm afraid so." She cast a furtive glance toward the closed door. "Someday, I'll have to tell you about Eric."

Someday? Adam's mind echoed the idea. Sara was talking as if they had a future together. That was pure fallacy. Yet he could see why she'd fallen into the trap of thinking their unique relationship would continue. There was already a kind of natural camaraderie between them. It sprang from the amiable rivalry of two corresponding intellects.

Talking with Sara was an adventure for his mind; one which he was thoroughly enjoying in spite of himself. He'd be willing to bet she was, too.

Which meant nothing. Adam strummed an opening chord and began to sing a plaintive ballad. By the third song, Sara's eyes had closed and she'd dozed off, slouched in a chair she'd pulled close to the fire. He would have covered her with a blanket and left her there if he hadn't been worried she might accidently get burned. Laying the guitar aside, he approached.

"Sara?" The shadows of her long, pale lashes

fluttered. Her eyes opened slowly, their depths misty and unfocused. She began to smile. Adam was pleased to see that she'd recognized him immediately.

"Oops." Her groggy expression grew apologetic. "I didn't mean to nod off. Your singing was wonderful. It's just that this has been a long, trying day." Not to mention the weeks and months preceding it, she added silently.

"No problem." He glanced toward the narrow bed. "I suppose you'd like to turn in."

Sara's strong sense of fairness surfaced. "I'm not taking your bed, if that's what you mean. I'll just make myself a pallet here on the floor, next to the fire where it's warm."

"You'll do nothing of the kind."

She was wholly awake, now, her stubbornness in full flower. Getting to her feet she faced him, hands on her hips. "Who says?"

"I do. Not only is this my house, I'm a lot bigger than you are."

"But I have Samson on my side." Sara reached down to lay her hand atop the dog's broad head and ruffle his silky ears. "Don't I, boy?" The dog snuggled against her legs, his thick fur fluffier than usual due to the vigorous towel drying he'd received.

"I wouldn't count on him to stay loyal," Adam warned. "All I have to do is open the door to the refrigerator and he'll be all mine again, heart and soul.''

"Just like a male. Always thinking about his stomach, right?''

Adam huffed. "Well, he didn't get that big without considerable help from me.''

"I suppose not.'' She gave the dog another affectionate pat. "I can see he'd have turned out to be a Chihuahua if you hadn't taken such good care of him when he was a puppy.''

"You're not going to distract me by making a joke out of it.'' Adam had to stifle the smile brought on by the image of Samson as a lap dog. "You get the bed. End of discussion.''

"But where will you sleep?''

The moment she uttered the innocent question Sara felt her cheeks begin to burn. This was the awkward moment she had anticipated. Yes, she trusted her host—sort of—yet she felt compelled to remind him of her strong moral code. The problem was finding a way to express herself clearly without sounding as if she were preaching.

Adam remained firm. "I plan to sleep on the floor.''

"I didn't mean to imply…'' She broke off, unsure of how to proceed.

"You don't have to apologize.'' He pulled extra blankets out of the chest at the foot of the bed. "And you don't have to explain. I already know you weren't inviting me to bunk with you."

"That's a relief."

"Does it surprise you?"

"A little." Remaining near the warm stove she folded her arms across her chest and hugged herself for extra emotional support.

"Well, it shouldn't. I'm usually a pretty good judge of people."

"Usually?" Sara wished she could say the same for herself.

"Yeah. Sometimes I goof big time." Like when I relaxed my guard and got Gene killed, he thought sadly.

Sara noticed Adam's gaze dart for an instant to the box of clothing peeking out from under the bed. The place where he'd gotten the jeans she was wearing. Evidently, his reference to making a mistake had to do with whoever had once belonged to the expensive things. Which was a conundrum in itself. Anyone who could afford such luxuries would be seriously out of place in Adam Callahan's austere life.

With a sigh, Sara crossed to the bed and perched, exhausted, on its edge, hands folded, shoulders slumped. "Okay, you win."

"Good." Adam regarded her quiet capitulation with puzzlement. "Are you all right?"

"Sure." She yawned. "I was just thinking."

"About what?" He busied himself making a pallet on the opposite side of the stove.

"About misjudging people. Apparently, you and I have that in common, too."

"Too? What else is there?" He peered around the side of the portly black stove.

"Well, for one thing, Samson likes us both. Which naturally means he must be a really intelligent animal."

"Come to think of it, you're right. I probably should have paid more attention to his opinion in the past." He paused, thoughtful. "Good night, Sara."

Fully dressed she crawled under the covers and pulled them up around her chin. "Good night, Adam." A silly bit of nostalgia popped into her mind and she added, "Good night, Grandpa, good night, John-Boy."

Adam muttered softly as he padded across the floor to turn out the lights. Sara managed to stay awake barely long enough to thank God for her rescue and the kindness of the stranger who had taken her in. Before she was through praying she had fallen soundly asleep.

It was a nudge from Samson's wet nose that roused her the following morning. Opening her eyes, Sara found him staring at her from barely six inches away. The effect was startling. So was his doggy breath!

Wide-eyed, she sucked in air to fuel a scream before she fully realized where she was. Or what kind of creature she was facing.

From across the room she heard a facetious, "Good morning. You going to sleep till noon?"

"I'm on vacation," Sara countered. "Cut me some slack."

Adam snorted. Apparently, his guest was *not* a morning person. "Yes, ma'am. Do you always wake up with such a sunny disposition?"

"No. Sometimes I'm much worse. What time is it, anyway?"

"Pretty late. Almost seven."

With a theatrical moan, Sara ducked down and pulled the comforter up over her face. Samson, however, was not about to let his new playmate hide from him. He immediately began to root under the edge of the blankets with his broad nose, coming up inside the bedclothes next to Sara's face.

"Aagh!" She bolted out of bed. Landing on the floor in her bare feet she glared at Adam. "You stinker! You put him up to that!"

"Not me. You're the one who petted and fussed over him yesterday. If he's spoiled, it's your fault."

Sara stood there in a half stupor and ran her fingers through her tangled hair. She never had been able to deal amiably with morning. This day was no different. Only the debt of gratitude which she owed her rescuer was keeping her from being a certified, card-carrying sourpuss.

She padded softly across the room. Adam was up to his midforearms in suds from the dishes they hadn't taken the time to wash the night before. The man was too good to be real. "I don't suppose you've got a spare cup of coffee?"

"Not till we stoke the wood stove, again. I'm running low on diesel and I'm not sure when I'll be able to get into town. I shut down the generator."

"Oh, dear. What about the refrigerator?"

"It'll stay cold if we don't open it too often." He shot her a condescending look. "You want coffee, go out to the woodshed, get an armload of dry kindling, and I'll build you a fire."

"Me?"

"You're the one who wants hot coffee, remember?" He snatched his recently used mug off the sink and dunked it in the dishwater before she could take notice. He'd brewed instant coffee in the microwave just before cutting the power. It was a wonder she hadn't smelled the tantalizing aroma.

Sara was a bright woman. Adam figured she'd realize he was teasing long before she made the trek to the shed. After all, he was washing the dishes in hot water. And the antique cookstove was propane powered with a manual ignition, so it required no electricity at all. He stifled a smile. Until she woke up all the way, figured out he was kidding, and told him off, it was fun to watch the disgruntled look she was trying to hide. To see the sparks of indignation in her hazel eyes.

''I don't believe this.'' She gave up trying to remain cordial, stomped off to the bathroom, and slammed the door behind her.

It took Sara only a few minutes of private prayer and serious contemplation to convince herself she was being unfair to her host. He had taken her in when she was in dire circumstances and had been as nice as can be since then, give or take the odd wisecrack. If it was dry firewood he needed, she'd get it. Without complaint.

She eased open the door and peeked out. Adam still stood at the sink, his back to her. Samson was nowhere to be seen.

She cast a sad glance at her soggy, ruined sandals. There was no use bothering with shoes. Judging by what she had seen through the bathroom window, the sun was out and the well-worn path to the shed was clear. The trip was a short one. Bare feet would be considerably easier to clean than shoes—if she'd had any others to sacrifice. She'd do this for Adam. Because she owed him that much, and more. And because she needed to make it up to him for grumbling without cause.

The cabin door creaked as she opened it and

ducked out. Behind her, she heard Adam shout, "Wait!"

"I'll just be a minute. Ooh. Ah. Eesh!" Off the porch, Sara danced through the cold, slippery mud.

"Sara! Come here."

"I will, I will." Pausing at the woodshed she turned to look back. "How much of this stuff do we need?"

He was sorely tempted to say, "None," but held his peace. If his guest hadn't overcome her dour morning mood he didn't think she'd appreciate his little joke. Might not, anyway. He figured it was best to simply use whatever firewood she brought, rather than confess.

"I'll bring all I can carry, okay?"

"Okay. Just get in here before you catch pneumonia."

"Right." Loading her arms with the smallest diameter logs she could find, Sara started back to Adam. She was three steps from the safety of the dry porch when a bolt of white shot past. It knocked into her left leg. She teetered. Whirled. Spun like a leaf in a whirlwind.

"Aaah!" Unable to regain her balance, Sara felt herself start to fall. All she could think of was keeping the wood dry. She tried to pass it to Adam.

He lunged toward her, hoping to avert the impending calamity. It was far too late. For both of them. He slipped on the bottom step and went sailing through the air, shouting. "Look out!"

Any assistance Adam might have been able to render was thwarted by the jumble of limbs and sticks Sara literally threw his way. One particularly heavy piece nicked his temple, leaving him dazed. When he shook the sense back into his head he was kneeling at the foot of the porch steps in a tangle of bark, raw lumber, and slippery red clay.

Seated opposite, Sara was up to her back pockets in the same mud. "What happened?"

"I think Samson wanted in."

She shook her hands at arm's length like a kitten with its paw dipped in the milk bowl. "Ugh. Remind me to give him the right-of-way the next time."

"No kidding." Adam tried to subdue his wide grin. He failed. "You should see yourself."

"You're no prize, either, mister," Sara retorted, giggling in spite of herself. She sobered. "What happened to your head?"

"My head?" He gingerly lifted one muddy hand, then decided it would be wiser to not touch the injury until he'd washed.

"It's bleeding."

"I'm sure I'll live." Adam got cautiously to his feet and held out his hand. "Come on. I owe you a cup of coffee."

"But, what about building a fire, first?" Clearly,

her efforts at gathering wood to stoke the stove had failed.

"We'll make do."

Taking his strong hand she let him help her to her feet. She'd expected him to let go as soon as she was upright. He didn't. The sense of safety in his warm, dynamic touch was far more soothing than she'd anticipated.

"You take a shower first," he said, penitent. "I'll have coffee waiting when you're done."

"You're probably going to have to lend me more clothes. I'm really sorry about the jeans. I'm afraid they'll never be the same."

"Neither will I," Adam muttered.

Sara gave no indication she'd heard what he said. He was still holding her hand. She loved the sympathetic gesture. It made her feel as secure as if she were enfolded in a tender embrace.

Her cheeks warmed. She averted her gaze. Her fingers slipped between his and she gave his hand a gentle squeeze. Never be the same? Boy, no kidding!

And he wasn't the only one affected that way. No matter what else happened, she'd never be the same, either. Not now that she'd met Adam Callahan.

Chapter Four

The aroma of coffee greeted Sara the moment she left the bathroom. Adam handed her a steaming mug, stuffed his hands in his pockets, and backed off discretely.

"Umm. That's better," she said, cradling the mug in both hands. She took a sip, smiled. "How did you manage?"

"It's an old-fashioned, homesteader secret."

Sara envisioned his blue-and-white enameled coffee pot buried in the smoldering ashes of the woodstove or hanging from a hook over an open fire. Curious, she pressed him for details. "Tell me. I'd love to have some genuine pioneer lore to share with my students this coming school year."

Clearing his throat, Adam decided to confess. "I made it on the stove. It's propane fired."

She was certain her gas stove at home required an electrical connection, too. "But, how...?"

He reached into a kitchen drawer and took out a red-handled tool that looked like a wand with a trigger. "You light the burners with this. A match would do the job, too, but this igniter is easier. It works like a cigarette lighter, only the flame comes out the end of a long snout so you don't get burned."

Sara was still hoping she hadn't been as dimwitted as she was beginning to think. She scowled. "But, last night you heated dinner in the wood stove. I thought..."

"The chicken and potatoes were already cooked and the coals in the stove were perfect for warming everything when we got back. I just thought you'd get a kick out of eating a meal that had been roasted on the coals in a Dutch oven. I never meant to imply that I couldn't have done the same thing on the stove."

Sara's mouth gaped, then snapped shut in indignation. What a fool she'd been. "And you thought it would be fun to send me out into the mud for firewood? What did I ever do to you?"

"Outside of half drown me and totally disrupt my peace and quiet? Nothing," he countered, trying a wry smile to see if she'd respond.

"You're forgetting alienation of affections," she snapped. "I've thoroughly ruined your dog."

Adam cocked an eyebrow at Samson, who had made straight for his favorite spot by the stove and laid down to lick his wet paws. He always did the same thing, whether there was a fire burning or not. "To tell you the truth, that mutt was already pretty spoiled. I've been trying to teach him not to barge through doors ever since he was a pup."

"Your dog training techniques could use some serious improvement."

"I guess my houseguest etiquette could, too."

"You said it. I didn't."

"No, but you were thinking it."

That, and a lot more, Sara admitted, blushing and looking away. She didn't want to dwell on how much she liked Adam, nor did she intend to let him know it. There were a few logistical problems, however, which she felt were safe topics for discussion.

Sipping her coffee, she enjoyed its familiar warmth while she formulated her latest idea, then spoke. "What I do think is that I've worn out my welcome. You've been more than generous, sharing your cabin and your food and all, but I ought to be on my way."

"Is someone expecting you?"

She decided it wouldn't hurt to tell him that much. "No. Nobody's lived on the old place since my great-grandmother died. I just meant it's time for me to go."

"Okay. I agree. Now, how do you propose to accomplish that?'' Adam leaned against the sink, his arms folded across his chest.

''Well, the rain's stopped. We'll just hike back to the car and…''

''We?''

Sara set her cup on the table and faced him, hands on her hips. ''Yes, *we*. It's either that or I camp here for the rest of the summer.''

''Heaven forbid.''

''Probably. At least I hope so.''

He was a little surprised that she'd taken his clichéd comment seriously. Then he recalled what she'd said about being a Christian and vowed to watch his references to that kind of thing in the future.

Sara went on, ''The trouble is, I have absolutely no idea how to get back to my car. You dragged me through the woods in the dead of night in the middle of a hurricane. There's no way I'm going to be able to backtrack by myself.'' She threw her hands up in frustration. ''I don't even know which direction to go to start looking.''

''It's too soon.''

''Too soon for what?'' She frowned at him.

Adam scowled back at her. ''It's going to be at least two or three days before anybody can negotiate the roads up here, even with a four-wheel-drive truck like mine.''

"Meaning?" Sara mirrored his stance, her arms folded, her back stiff.

"Meaning, we're stuck here. Just you, me and the dog. A real happy family."

"That's impossible. Surely, you can call me a tow truck or something."

Acting far more nonchalant than he felt, Adam shrugged. "Look. Tell you what we'll do. I don't have a phone. As soon as I'm sure the weather will hold, we'll hike down to the mom-and-pop grocery store at Flatrock and see if we can get somebody to come up and pull you out."

"Somebody professional? I'd hate to damage my rental car, even though it isn't new."

"You should have thought of that before you drove it off the road," he countered.

"Actually, I was trying to see if it would float," she quipped dryly. "But it got stuck on the berm before I could make it all the way to the river, below." Sara saw her rescuer's countenance darken.

"Don't make jokes like that," he warned. "Life-threatening situations aren't funny."

"I never said they were. I was just..." The look in his eyes kept her from continuing. Something or someone in Adam's past must have contributed greatly to his negative response. That wasn't her fault. However, she could tell he was clearly beyond accepting any innocent attempts at humor so she backed off and faced him soberly.

"Look, I'm sorry if I offended you. All my life, I've tended to make jokes out of all kinds of situations, even the most desperate ones. I guess it's my way of coping. I don't mean anything bad by it."

She paused, studying his closed expression and trying to guess what made him tick. "Before you came up here and shut yourself away like this, were you a doctor or an ambulance driver or something?"

He shook his head slowly, his blue gaze capturing hers and holding it as securely as if he'd taken her hands and was forcing her to look at him. "No," he said, voice low and rumbling. "I was a cop."

The rain resumed by lunchtime. Sara had insisted they start the generator long enough for her to run a load of laundry through the washing machine perched on the narrow back porch. Her rationale was flawless. One more slide in the red clay of the yard and she'd be out of wearable clothing, not counting the unmentionables she had stuffed in her pack.

Using the dryer, however, was impossible in the wind-driven downpour, so they'd carted the damp, clean clothes inside and rigged up ropes as clotheslines to dry the wettest articles. By the time the laundry was hung, the tiny cabin reminded Sara of a soggy, ramshackle maze.

"I feel like a mouse," she called, ducking a stiffening pair of jeans located close to the stove's radiating heat and making her way toward Adam.

He threw a last bath towel over the rope and looked in the direction of her voice. "A what? Where's a mouse?"

Sara laughed lightly. "No. Not a real mouse. I mean, this arrangement feels like we're stuck in some kind of a bizarre maze."

"It's not normally this crowded in here when I have to resort to this method," he explained. "A pair of jeans and maybe a few towels by the stove is usually all I hang. It's a good thing the weather's stayed cold or we wouldn't have the heat from the stove to help dry this stuff."

She lifted the lower corner of another towel and peeked past it to smile up at him. "I really am sorry I inconvenienced you and disturbed your solitude."

"I'll live."

She swept aside the towel and stepped into the confining space between the row of laundry and the edge of the sink where Adam stood. "Don't you get lonely way out here? This is beautiful country and all, but I just think, I'd miss people."

Adam stared at her. The already humid air seemed suddenly rarified. The hanging laundry had enclosed the two of them in such a small space he couldn't help noticing everything about Sara. His oversize sweatshirt had never looked so good. She was attractive. Appealing. Almost endearing. He would have turned away and fled if there had been anywhere else to go. He finally found his voice. "I don't miss people at all."

"But you did, once, didn't you?" Sara's words were soft, gently spoken. Without realizing it, she'd drawn on her internal resources to express the spiritual love Adam needed. The love that he'd banished from his wounded soul.

He stiffened. Mentally withdrew. "I don't know how we got on this subject but let's drop it, okay? My life is none of your concern, so don't try fixing it."

That statement acted like a bucket of ice water in Sara's face, negating the compassion blossoming in her heart and refocusing her mind. If anybody's life needed fixing, it was hers. For the first time in hours she thought of Eric, remembered her earlier fear, wondered where he was and if she had truly escaped his uncalled-for interest.

She huffed. "You have absolutely nothing to worry about. If I could fix *any* life, I'd start with my own, thank you."

"Yours?" Adam was surprised. "From the things you've said and the way you've been kidding around, I'd have thought for sure you were happy."

"That's a subjective term," Sara countered. "If you'd asked me the same question six months ago, I'd have told you everything was perfect."

"And now?"

Her glance darted past Adam to the window

above the sink. Eric could be out there in the woods. Watching her. Hidden by the rain. Just waiting for his chance to get her alone, again. To scare her to death with his cool assurances that they were meant for each other no matter how many times she told him no.

Why God had allowed that charlatan to fool her—to fool everyone—so completely, was a mystery Sara still hadn't figured out. Maybe she never would. At this point, all she wanted was to be free of Eric Rydell. To be able to go to bed at night and not worry that he was stalking her.

She shivered, wrapped her arms around herself. "Now," she said quietly, answering Adam's query, "I just want to get to Grandma Stone's homestead. I need time to think."

"Alone?" Adam asked perceptively.

"Yes," Sara said. "Alone."

It was later in the day before Adam decided to broach the subject of his guest's uneasiness again. The laundry had dried, thanks to the added heat from the wood stove, and the cabin was no longer so crowded it felt claustrophobic. He'd noted that Sara had relaxed appreciably, though she probably wouldn't stay that way for long. Not once he started asking questions. He fully intended to cross-examine her until he found out who or what she was afraid of.

She'd found a paperback mystery to read and was curled up comfortably by the fire, apparently ignoring him. If Adam hadn't been trained to notice nuances of body language and details of his surroundings he might have actually believed she wasn't paying attention to anything but her reading.

He pulled a ladder-back chair close to her and sat down. "Sara?"

Blinking, she looked up. "Yes?"

"You've been on the same page of that book for the past twenty minutes. Either you're a very slow reader or you have something else on your mind. Would you like to talk about it?"

The query caught her off guard. "You're very perceptive."

"It's the ex-cop in me."

"Umm...I see." Thoughtful, she considered the current situation. Maybe she'd been wrong to think God had abandoned her, had ignored her prayers for deliverance. Maybe He'd been in charge all along and had brought her to Adam Callahan for protection. The idea had enough merit to give her waning faith a needed boost.

She studied Adam's face, looking for clues to the Lord's supposed plans, trying to decide whether or not she should confide in someone she'd just met. She began to smile.

"What's so funny?" he asked.

"Me. I was sitting here, wondering if I should

trust you with my problems, when it occurred to me I'd already put my life in your hands. If you hadn't come along when you did, I could have been seriously injured. Or worse.''

"Well, I wouldn't go quite that far."

"I would. Think about it. My car could have slid over the cliff. If I'd made it to the bottom of the chasm in one piece I still could have drowned in the river. Or, I could have been struck by lightning." Or Eric could have caught up to me, she added, silently. "Any number of horrible things could have happened…and didn't.''

He chuckled. "I can't take credit for all that, I'm afraid.''

"No. But I'd been praying for help before you showed up. That gives you pretty good references as far as I'm concerned.''

Adam leaned back, shook his head. "Oh, no. Don't go imagining I'm some kind of guardian angel. I told you, I don't believe in that kind of stuff.''

"You said you did once, though, right?''

"Did I say that?'' He made a face. "Okay. Maybe I did. That doesn't mean I'm a part of some divine rescue squad. If there is a God, which I seriously doubt, He and I haven't been on speaking terms for a long time.''

Sara recalled a Bible verse in the book of John about no one being able to steal a soul from Christ that already belonged to Him. Between her own recent doubt and lack of faith, and Adam's denial of any faith at all, the verse became doubly meaningful.

"Have it your way," Sara said. "You'll never convince me I didn't stumble into your neck of the woods for a reason." Her gaze darted to the window, then back, swift as a hawk in pursuit of its prey.

Nevertheless, Adam noticed. "Who do you think is out there?"

"What makes you think...?" She stopped the pretext before it went any further and waved her hands in surrender. "Sorry. I'm so used to making excuses it's gotten to be a habit, I guess." This man was a cop. A professional. Sara reasoned it wouldn't hurt to tell him a little about what had driven her from her home and sent her on a quest for both peace of mind and a renewal of her tattered faith. Besides, he might actually believe her. No one else had.

Patient, Adam waited, watched her internal struggle. He was rewarded in a few moments.

"It all started around Christmastime," Sara said. "We had an unexpected vacancy in the sixth grade and the school district hired a man named Eric Rydell to fill it."

"Is that who has you so spooked?"

"Yes." She sighed and began shaking her head in self-derision. "He seemed like the perfect man. So polite. So refined. I wasn't the only one who was fooled. Everybody liked him. The mistake I made was seeing him socially.''

"You dated?'' Adam wished he could take notes but decided that might be too off-putting, so he simply listened and committed the details to memory. Later, if necessary, he'd ask Sara to repeat portions of her story.

"In a way. We mostly confined our meetings away from school to an occasional dinner or a movie. I even took him to church with me and introduced him to all my Christian friends. Our relationship wasn't anything hot and heavy, like the stuff you see on prime-time television.'' Her cheeks warmed, reddened. "That's one of the things that made me so mad. When I went to the police, they treated me like Eric and I'd had some kind of a lover's quarrel.''

It was the telltale moisture pooling in her eyes that made Adam reach out and pat the back of her hand for reassurance. "Go on. When did he turn mean?''

Sara's eyes widened. "How did you know?''

"A lucky guess. Keep talking.''

"It started slowly. There was something about being with him that felt wrong. As if God were trying to warn me. But I was a fairly new believer and I thought maybe I was imagining things. Folks at church seemed perfectly at ease with him, which confused me even more. So, I decided to stop seeing him for a while.'' She paused, blinking back tears at the remembrance.

"He didn't like the idea."

"Boy, no kidding! I've never seen such a change come over anyone. It was like he'd been hiding this sinister side of his personality. He threatened me— actually threatened me."

"What did he say?"

Sara's hands were trembling. She closed them into fists in her lap. "Nothing really specific. Just that I couldn't break up with him and that he'd see to it I was sorry if I tried. It was more the hateful *way* he said it than the actual words. That, and the cold, menacing look in his eyes."

Adam was getting more and more uneasy as her story unfolded. There was no way to tell for sure without a psychological profile of Rydell, but the man sounded as if he could be seriously unbalanced. Dangerous. Which meant Sara Stone was probably in a lot more trouble than she thought.

Leaning forward, his elbows resting on his knees, Adam folded his hands and struck a pose meant to relax his companion while his own adrenaline surged and his body readied for battle the way it always had when he was on the force. "Lots of men get mad when they're rejected," he said calmly. "What did Rydell do next?"

Sara huffed. "Do? Nothing, on the surface. He was as pleasant and perfect as always, anytime there were witnesses. It was enough to make me sick. I thought, if I just stuck to my decision, he'd eventually get tired of glaring at me at work and move on to somebody else. Only he didn't. He started showing up at my house at all hours and sitting in his car, watching every move I made.''

Adam was getting agitated. "There are laws against stalking. Did you report it?''

"Of course I did!'' She jumped to her feet and began pacing the small cabin. "Nobody believed me. It was as if the whole world bought his Mr. Perfect act and I was just some nut who couldn't get along with her long-suffering boyfriend.''

"So you ran.'' Adam straightened, shrugged. "I can see why you'd think that would help.''

"I didn't do it because I thought it was right,'' Sara told him. "I did it because I couldn't just sit there and take it anymore. Everybody treated me as if Eric were the victim and I was too blind to see what a wonderful man he was!''

At wit's end, she turned away from Adam so he couldn't see her tears of frustration. Rehashing her problems had made them seem more real, more alarming. Worse...if that was possible.

Adam approached slowly, tentatively, intending only to soothe her with his words, not to touch her. He knew what it was like to stand alone in a war with evil. He knew what it was like to lose, too. If there was any way to do it, he intended to see that Sara Stone won her battle.

Speaking evenly, his voice low, he said simply, "I believe you."

When she gasped, whirled, and fell into his arms, sobbing with relief, he did the only thing he could. He held her until she was through crying.

Chapter Five

Sara would have been a lot more embarrassed by her loss of self-control if it hadn't felt so right to accept solace from Adam Callahan. There was something about him that inspired confidence. Made her feel acceptable for the first time in ages.

He hadn't teased or cajoled her afterward, either. He'd merely allowed her to be herself, without pretext and without conforming to predetermined ideas of how she should behave. She hadn't felt that free since she'd walked the aisle at church to declare her faith!

Best of all, he hadn't mentioned her emotional outburst since it had happened. Neither had she. It was enough to know he took her concerns seriously. Evidence of that was in his changed behavior. He'd become wary, watching, just as she'd been, and had even left the house to rig up a trip wire around the perimeter of the clearing in which the cabin stood. Now they'd be forewarned if anyone came near.

By afternoon, the rain had stopped and there was actually sunshine peeking though the tops of the trees. Adam pointed it out. "Looks like we can count on a few hours of nice weather."

"I'm glad." Eager for the respite, Sara went to the window. "Is there any way we could go outside for a while?" She'd been feeling cooped up inside the small cabin, especially since Adam's innocent expression of tenderness, and she craved a diversion.

"You can go anywhere you want. Just open the door."

She made a silly face. "I know that. I meant, do you think it's safe?"

"Knowing how you like to slide around in the mud, probably not," he joked, purposely avoiding any mention of the man she feared. "But we did do laundry, so you'll have a dry change of clothes for the next time you take a dive."

"Very funny."

"Actually, it was." He grinned. "I didn't say so at the time because you'd already conked me with a log. I figured there was more where that came from if I made you mad." He gently touched the cut on his forehead.

"Are you okay? Really?"

"I'm fine. I've had worse and lived."

"I suppose we all have." She drew on childhood memories for comparison. "When I was about five years old, I crawled out a second-story window to see a bird's nest in the gutters of my house and nearly killed myself. At least, that's what my mother claimed."

Adam chuckled. "I can see you doing that. Where was that? Around here?"

"No. In a suburb of Chicago."

"Well, well. I used to live up there, too. Did your family move to Arkansas later?"

"No. I only came here when I visited my great-grandma Stone. She took me in one summer when I was about six or seven. That was when I fell in love with this part of the country."

Sara sighed in remembrance. "When I finally went home to Illinois, all excited and ready to tell my parents what a wonderful adventure I'd had, my folks were separated and my daddy was gone. Nothing was ever the same after that. And I never got to come back to see my granny while she was still living."

What a shame. "Well, you're here now," Adam reminded her. "So let's make the most of it. I think the good weather will hold long enough for us to get down to the grocery store and back if we hurry. It's not far."

"I thought you said the roads were impassible."

"Roads?" he quipped. "Who said anything about roads?"

Sara wore her soggy sandals for want of anything more practical. According to Adam, they didn't have time to walk to the nearest phone and make the side trip to her car for her sneakers, too. Besides, she'd have had to wear the sandals until she'd retrieved her other shoes, anyway.

Following him through the leaf-strewn forest with Samson ranging on ahead, she stepped into a hidden depression and felt cold goo ooze between her toes. "Ugh! Eesh!"

Adam glanced over his shoulder. "What's your problem?"

Sara was precariously balanced on one foot and shaking the other. "I need boots."

"Or fisherman's waders," he cracked back. "Those reach all the way to above your waist. It should help with your mud fixation."

"I don't have a fixation," she argued. "It *is* muddy out here."

He laughed. "Okay, it's muddy. I hope you don't expect me to carry you."

"Of course not. I'm perfectly capable of walking."

"Good, because that would slow us down too much."

She gave up trying to get the sticky wet goo out

from between her toes and faced him squarely. "How much farther is it to the store? It doesn't look like there's a settlement for miles."

"The Ozarks can be deceiving. They aren't high mountains, like the Rockies, but they hold all kinds of secrets. You'll find small communities in places you'd never dream they'd be."

"Okay. If you say so. I just wish I didn't get turned around so easily out here. I don't have the foggiest idea which way is home."

"Home?"

"A figure of speech."

"Oh. Well, fortunately, I never get lost, so you're in good hands."

She stifled the urge to comment. *Good hands* wasn't the half of it. She's already noticed a new sense of well-being while in Adam's company. A sense of safety, as if her Heavenly Father had known exactly what she needed and had provided it in spite of her headstrong insistence that she could handle her own muddled affairs by simply running away from her problems.

They were climbing a steep hill and weaving between short, bushy cedar trees and taller oaks. Busy spiders had festooned the sunny spaces between the trees but fortunately, Adam's broad-shouldered bulk swept the harmless animals out of the way before Sara got there. She spent half the time making sure her footing was secure and the other half admiring the man walking ahead of her to break trail. He moved like a natural athlete and his shoulder-length hair just begged her to touch its softness, to run her fingers through the slight curl at the ends.

Breathless, she joined him at the crest of a ridge. "Whew! That was a workout. I wouldn't need to take an aerobics class if I lived out here."

He laughed. "The local folks would probably think you were crazy if you suggested such a thing. They work hard, play hard and rest with just as much gusto. Exercise for its own sake probably isn't a concept they'd understand."

"I never did, either, really. It always seemed to me there must be some job that needed doing where I could use my excess energy to accomplish something useful."

"Oh, good," Adam teased. "I have a pile of wood that needs splitting."

Sara shot him a wry smile. "Don't hold your breath, mister. I was just being philosophical."

"It figures." He pointed. "Look down there. Where Samson's headed. See the white building? That's the Flatrock store I told you about."

"It's darling! Looks like a postcard."

"*Quaint* is probably a more apt description. The place isn't fancy but it has a phone and provisions. Right now, that's all we need."

All we need? Sara seriously doubted that. She'd already grasped parallels between her life and

Adam's. It was easy to imagine that he'd been sent to help her. In the back of her mind a new hunch was stirring. Was it possible that she was also meant to help *him?*

She stared at his strong back as he started down the hill toward the store. How did God expect her to help the man when she had no idea what was bothering him, what had caused him to renounce his faith? The few times he'd alluded to his past he'd behaved as if he were angry, then abruptly changed the subject. The last thing she needed in her life was another troubled individual like Eric. A man who hid his true feelings.

Besides, she had so little faith left herself, she'd be crazy to think she had enough to share.

The Flatrock grocery, with living quarters above, was more like an old-fashioned general mercantile than it was a food store. Half the wooden building was devoted to clothing like overalls, flannel shirts and rainwear, plus fishing lures and mottled brown gear intended for hunters. The other half of the room held mostly canned goods and staples like flour and sugar. Adam had been right when he'd described the place as a piece of history. From the moment Sara had stepped onto the wooden porch and entered through the weathered screen door, she'd felt transported back in time to the forties or fifties. Even the soda pop machine was antiquated. Narrow-necked bottles slid along a metal track to a catch at the end, which released them when the right coins were dropped into the pay slot.

Adam greeted the taciturn proprietor, Farley Burnham, and introduced him to Sara. Left outside, Samson sat at the door and whined for admittance.

Smiling her best smile, Sara nodded politely to the portly, older man. "Pleased to meet you." His only response was a reserved nod.

"Any mail for me?" Adam asked.

Farley scratched his balding head. "Not today. Expectin' some?"

"Just the usual. I'm going to go use the pay phone." He glanced briefly at Sara. "Rest. Look around. You may find something you need."

"Probably. I *need* just about everything right now." Under the watchful eye of the storekeeper, she began to wander among the tables and shelves overflowing with merchandise. "You have a wonderful store, Mr. Burnham."

He hooked his thumbs through the shoulder straps of his denim overalls, rocked on his heels, puffed out his chest proudly, and acknowledged the compliment. "Might as well call me Farley. Everybody does. You're not from around here, are you?"

"No." She'd noticed that Adam's voice often took on a hint of the local southern accent. She had no such natural advantage to help her blend in. "I suppose you can tell, huh?"

"Yup. Pretty much. Where you'ns from?"

Stifling a smile at the colloquialism, she wondered why he hadn't said, *y'all,* the way she'd expected. Her teacher's brain decided the difference must be that one form was singular and the other, plural. How interesting. "I was raised near Chicago," she said, quickly adding, "but my Granny Stone had a place not far from here."

"The old Euless Stone place?"

"Yes. You knew her?"

"Not personally. Her people are kin to my wife's family, though. Guess that makes you and me kin, too."

"Yes, I guess it does." Sara was elated at the connection, however obscure. It made her feel more a part of the Ozarks, the way she had as a child.

She picked up a pair of black rubber boots and carried them with her through the store while she looked for thick socks. Most of her traveling money was still back in the car but she'd stashed a little cash in the backpack she'd left at Adam's cabin. All she'd need was a small cash advance from him and she wouldn't have to slog through the mud practically barefooted anymore. What a pleasant thought.

When she found him leaning on the wall in the rear of the store, still speaking on the pay phone, she accosted him excitedly. "Oh, good! Is that the tow truck? Can they pull me out soon?"

He waved a hand to quiet her. "Hush."

"Okay." Sara made a face at him. "Be a grouch. I can wait." Listening, she was surprised to hear him talking like a cop.

"I want a complete rundown on the guy," Adam was saying. "That's right. Go back as far as you need to. It's Rydell. Eric Rydell." He spelled the whole name, then looked to Sara for confirmation.

She clutched the rubber boots to her chest and nodded silently.

"Okay. You have this number. Farley can reach me if it's an emergency. I'll check back in a few days."

When he hung up, she asked, "Do you really think that was necessary? I mean, maybe Eric's just too possessive. You said some men are like that."

"I know what I said."

Sara studied his closed expression, his firm jaw. One phone call to his old friends on the force and he'd become another person. A formidable adversary. She supposed she should be thankful to have such a determined champion. She wasn't ungrateful. Not really. She just wanted her amiable companion back.

In the end, Adam bought Sara boots, extra socks, a few additional supplies and a treat for Samson. Given a choice, she would have added more chocolate to their provisions. It never hurt to have a candy bar or two in reserve for emergencies.

"Next time, I'll remember to bring my pack so we can carry the groceries home in it," she volunteered.

"Next time?"

"When we come down to order the tow truck."

"I did that already."

His matter-of-fact tone saddened her. It didn't surprise her, though. She was only his guest because of extenuating circumstances, not because he'd actually invited her to camp in his house. Of course he wanted to be rid of her.

She trudged along behind him up the hill. The boots and thick, padded socks were a bit cumbersome. "When did the tow truck people say they could get to my car?"

Adam glanced at the sky, noted the gray clouds blowing across the sun. "Probably in a few days. Weather's unpredictable up here. Sometimes we get a lot of rain all at once, like now. The only thing we can do is wait and see." A drop of water hit his head as if to punctuate his statement. "Looks like it's going to start coming down again. We'd better hurry."

"I've *never* been as wet as I have since I got here," Sara said, having to almost run to keep up with his longer, practiced strides. "Or as muddy."

He laughed. "You did look pretty bad."

"Thanks a lot," she said, feigning ire. She cast a wary eye toward the darkening sky. "Do you think

I'll need that disposable plastic poncho you bought me?''

''Not if we don't stand around talking.''

She hustled to catch up to him once again, stepping in his footprints whenever possible, knowing she'd find firm ground there. ''I'm not standing. I'm doing the best I can. Your legs are just longer so you can take bigger steps. It's not my fault I'm short.''

Stepping over a fallen tree limb she lunged, stumbled in the cumbersome boots, then recovered. With her mind on keeping pace, she didn't stop to censor her mental rambling before she spoke. ''Now that we're on the subject of me being smaller than you are, whose jeans am I wearing?''

Adam stopped walking. Stiffened. Sara caught up to him and looked into his telling expression, then rued her loose tongue. ''I'm sorry,'' she said quickly. ''I know it's none of my business. I shouldn't have asked. Forget I said anything.''

As if he could forget anything she said or did. Ever. ''It's all right.'' He hesitated a moment longer. ''The clothes belonged to Gene.''

She sensed that this woman, whoever she was, had come to some kind of sad end.

''Gene died five years ago,'' Adam said flatly. ''I just never bothered to get rid of the clothes.'' Regaining control of his turbulent emotions he started to walk on.

Empathy filled her. Motivated her to say, "I'm really sorry." For a few minutes she didn't think her companion was going to respond. When he did, there was a telling catch in his voice.

"It's okay." Adam cleared his throat. "It was a long time ago." When Sara laid a comforting hand on his arm, he was so moved by her unquestioned compassion that tears filled his eyes.

Samson beat them home. Tongue lolling, the dog was lying on the porch when Adam arrived. Adam glanced over his shoulder to look for Sara and was surprised to see her limping up to the edge of the clearing.

"What happened to you?" he called back.

"Big rain boots," she gasped. "Turned my ankle."

"Well, why didn't you say so?"

"I can make it."

Grumbling to himself, Adam trotted back to where she was leaning against a white oak, trying to catch her breath. "Have you always been so stubborn?"

"So they tell me. Whew! I've found muscles I didn't even know I had."

"Wait till tomorrow. You'll be well acquainted."

"No kidding." Her breath was ragged, her fatigue evident.

"I'm sorry if I broke trail too fast. I'm so used

to hiking these hills I guess I forgot that you're new at this.''

"Not for long," Sara said with a wry grin. "I should be ancient real soon. I can feel old age gaining on me by the minute."

Adam chuckled, bent down and scooped her up in his arms. "Okay. I'll tote you the rest of the way."

"Oh, sure. Now you volunteer. When we're within spitting distance of your front door. Some knight in shining armor you are."

He paused. Held her slightly away from his chest. "You want me to drop you right here?"

"No!" Sara squealed, giggling. Wrapping an arm around his neck, she clung tightly. "No more mud. Please."

"Okay, okay. But you'd better stop calling me names if you want me to keep being nice to you."

"Yes, sir, Mr. Callahan, sir. You're clearly a prince among men. A real great guy. A—"

"All right. That's enough. I didn't mean you had to kiss up to me."

At the mention of the word *kiss,* Sara's breath caught. She was close enough to feel the hammering of Adam's heart through his flannel shirt, to sense the tensing of his muscles as he held her and he realized what he'd said.

She raised her eyes to search his, felt the whisper of his warm breath on her face. Her lips parted.

Trembled. For an instant the world consisted of only the two of them, wondering, waiting.

Sara sensed that the chance to share a kiss with Adam would soon pass. It might never again occur. That realization made it easier for her to tug slightly on his neck, to pull him a fraction of an inch closer. He didn't resist the way she'd feared he might.

Adam lowered his mouth to hers, meaning only to bestow a friendly kiss to celebrate their blossoming camaraderie. He was fooling himself. One touch of Sara's sweet lips and he lost all belief in his ability to limit his emotional involvement. Even as he deepened the kiss, he called himself every kind of a fool for permitting it to happen.

How dumb could he get? First, he'd let his sense of duty push him into getting tangled up in her problems with Eric Rydell when he had no authority to do so. Then, he'd given in to a stupid whim and made romantic overtures he had no intention of continuing. It didn't get any worse than that. Not with his past record. Being too close to Adam Callahan wasn't smart for anybody. Just look what it had cost his brother, Gene.

Adam abruptly broke contact and set Sara on her feet.

Starry-eyed, she gazed up at him. One hand remained on his shoulder to steady herself. Amazed, she sighed and whispered, "Oh, my…"

"Yeah." Muttering, he stepped farther away from her. "I didn't mean for that to happen."

She found his self-retribution ridiculous, given the obvious compatibility and like-mindedness they had just discovered, and she expressed her opinion with conspicuous sarcasm. "Oh, it wasn't so bad."

"Not bad?" One eyebrow arched.

Smiling knowingly she shrugged. "You know, as in fairly passable...considering."

"Considering what?"

It was funny how his standoffish attitude had mellowed since she'd begun belittling their kiss. "Considering the fact that you hated it so much."

"I never said..." Adam stopped himself from spelling out his thoughts but it was already too late to deny what he'd felt.

"That's what I figured," Sara said grinning. She pushed past him and climbed onto the porch, nudging Samson away from the front door so she could open it. "You'd better come on in, Adam. In case you haven't noticed, it's starting to rain, again. You're getting all wet."

Chapter Six

For the next few days, they settled into a simple routine that precluded close contact as much as possible. Adam read or puttered around outside the cabin, weather permitting. Sara played solitaire on her laptop until she was bored silly, then picked up the mystery novel she'd been trying to read, before.

For the sake of propriety, she'd offered repeatedly to go back to Burnham's General Store and ask to stay with the Burnhams until her car was freed from the muck. It worried her that she was beginning to like being around Adam too much for her own good. Yet each time she'd brought up the subject of leaving, he'd talked her out of it. For some reason, he seemed to feel responsible for her, even insisting that he was the only one who could adequately protect her if Eric had really followed. It wasn't until he took his ideas one step further that she fully understood the reasoning behind them.

"If Rydell is dangerous, what makes you think you'd be safe at the store?" Adam asked.

"He's always been okay when other people are around."

"Then think about *them*. Suppose he's changed since you ran away from him. Is it fair to place anybody else at risk?"

"I hadn't thought about it quite that way. You're right, of course." She hesitated. "I'm sorry you got dragged into this."

"Better me than old Farley. I'm used to sticking my neck out."

"Was it so bad? Being a cop, I mean."

"It had its rewarding moments. Most of the time it was pretty routine."

"Why did you quit?" She saw him wrestle with giving her a straight answer, then close his countenance as tightly as if he'd slammed the door to a bank vault and thrown away the lock's combination.

Getting to his feet, Adam skillfully changed the subject. "It's been two days since the last heavy downpour. Suppose we take my truck and drive down the hill to see if Farley's heard from my friends? After that, we can stop by your car and liberate some of your gear. That's better than waiting till a tow service can get to it."

The thought of clean clothes that actually fit

brightened Sara's mood appreciably. She jumped to her feet. "I'd *love* that. Just let me brush my hair and I'll be ready to go."

The idea of watching her brush her hair made Adam's skin tingle. She'd sat close to the stove the evening before, drying her freshly washed hair in the radiating heat, and he'd had to actually turn away to keep from taking her in his arms and kissing her again. If Sara didn't leave soon, the strain of having her around was bound to get to him. Wear him down.

And that would never do. Adam had realized, almost from the outset, that he needed to protect Sara from two dangers: Eric Rydell and himself. Rydell, he could handle. His own feelings were going to be harder.

Sara emerged from the bathroom, fresh-faced and eager. "Okay. I'm ready."

Amazed at his delight at her reappearance, Adam stared. How could anybody look so good in cast-off clothing and oversize rubber boots? The women he'd dated in the past had spent fortunes to create an elegant image, yet hadn't begun to approach the lovely, radiant appearance Sara seemed to acquire so naturally. Not only that, she was a joy to be around. There was a light in her eyes, a warmth to her heart that was unmistakable. Maybe that was the key.

She headed for the door. "Well? You coming? I definitely need a dose of sunshine."

You're my dose of sunshine, he realized with a start. That was the answer. Sara Stone had brightened his life simply by becoming a part of it. And the storm clouds would return, as surely as they filled the skies of the Ozarks every spring, because she'd leave. Adam knew it had to happen. It must. The surprising thing was, he didn't want her to go.

"I saw no need for a fancy, new truck when all I do is knock around up here in the woods," he explained, escorting her to the rear of the cabin and gesturing toward the old, green, four-wheel-drive vehicle parked there.

"You don't need to make excuses. I'm just glad we didn't have to hike to the store this time."

"You did fine on the trail. Really." To make sure she knew he meant the compliment, he added, "You're a pretty gutsy lady."

"Am I?" She was beaming. "You're not so bad, yourself."

"Thanks. I think."

Looking back at the cabin she asked, "Aren't we taking Samson?"

"Not this time. I want him here as a watchdog." He opened the passenger door for her. "Hop in."

Sara looked up at the height of the seat, then down at her feet. "I think *hop* is the right word.

How in the world am I supposed to get in there, take a flying leap?''

"You do it just like any other truck."

She eyed the wheels. "Are they *all* this tall?"

"The ones with four-wheel-drive sit higher," Adam said. He put out his hand. "Here. I'll help you."

"No, no." She waved him off. "If you can do it, I can do it. All I have to do is get one foot up that high and I've got it made. Stand back."

Only there was nothing to grab to give herself an initial lift, and even if there had been, her stiff, men's jeans didn't permit her to raise her right foot that high.

Determined to succeed, Sara decided to jump. She backed up, took two long strides, and launched herself before Adam could intervene.

He saw her start to get a grip on the edge of the door opening with her muddy boot, then slip. She threw her upper body over the end of the truck seat and clawed at the upholstery, trying to get a handhold.

"Hang on!" Reacting instinctively, Adam reached for her, hesitated, then changed his mind repeatedly, his hands waving in the empty air over her backside. No way was he going to grab her like that! Not even if it meant she'd wind up in the mud, again.

Sara landed feet first back on the ground with a

muffled, "Uumpf!" She immediately turned to Adam. "You were standing right there. You could have given me a hand."

"You said you could do it by yourself. Far be it from me to contradict a stubborn woman."

"Since when has that stopped you?" She noted that his face seemed flushed. "I almost made it. Why didn't you at least give me a boost?"

"Because I'm a gentleman," he countered. "If I'd grabbed you the way I'd have had to in order to catch you, you'd have conked me with another log. Guaranteed."

It suddenly occurred to Sara what kind of view she must have presented to him on her downward slide from the truck. No wonder he'd blushed. She softened her stance. "Okay. I think I see what you mean. You're forgiven. This time."

"How kind of you." Adam tried again. "*Now* will you let me give you a hand up?"

Sara nodded. The instant she placed her hand in his and sensed the emotional bond between them intensifying, she knew why she'd subconsciously declined his help, before. She and Adam Callahan were strangers, brought together by current circumstance and held together by nothing more. He was a recluse. A dropout from society. They had nothing in common. Not goals. Not life-styles. Not even their faith, considering his insistence he had none.

Even the simple touching of hands was ill-advised, given those facts. She'd made the mistake of getting involved with the wrong man, before, and look what had happened. Her intuition was already suspect, if not nonexistent. She wasn't about to trust it again.

Adam helped her into the truck, then released her immediately, as if taking her hand had meant nothing to him. Sara knew she should have been glad for his indifference, should have thanked God that the temptation she was feeling was one-sided. No matter how much she liked Adam, she wasn't going to let herself fall for him, so it was just as well that he had no romantic interest in her, right?

Right, she insisted, trying to make herself believe it. But she didn't. Not for a minute.

Thankfully, it was a lot farther to Flatrock by road than it had been when they'd cut cross-country. The longer trip gave Sara enough time to get control of her confusing emotions and tuck them away, returning to her usually cheerful disposition.

Adam pulled the truck to a stop in front of Burnham's General Store and got out. Before he could circle to the passenger side, Sara had already opened her door and jumped to the ground.

She glanced back at the seat and blushed, recalling the reason Adam had failed to give her a boost. "You need a ladder for that thing, you know."

"I'll get you a box," he gibed. "Any particular color you prefer?"

"Umm…" She struck a thinker's pose. "Muddy red clay and slimy-green would be nice. I like all my accessories to be color-coordinated."

"Around here, they call that camo. You know, short for camouflage. It's supposed to help hunters hide in the woods, but everybody wears it all the time. It's turned into common fashion in these parts."

Sara smiled. "You're supposed to say, 'In these *here* parts', if I remember right."

"In that case," Adam said with a wide grin, "I'm *fixin'* to go inside. You comin'?"

"Shore am. You can't get shut of me."

He laughed. "Very good. You're learning. Your granny'd be proud."

"She always said she was proud of me. She was quite a lady." Sara wiped her feet on the mat on the porch, then stood back so Adam could do the same. "I loved her dearly, even though I only got to be with her for a few months. She was the first person who took me to church, you know."

He held the door open for her. "Is that significant?"

"I think so. She planted the seeds of my faith, such as it is."

Adam wasn't about to engage in a discussion of the merits of religion in a public place like Farley's store. Most of the people in the area spoke of Christianity as if it were an integral part of their lives. That was one of the things he'd had to get used to when he'd moved out of the city, and in his case, he'd figured it was best to keep his negative opinions to himself. If a belief in God helped somebody get by, then that was their prerogative. As for him, he'd learned otherwise. The hard way.

Following Sara, Adam greeted the proprietor. "Morning, Farley."

"Mornin'. Y'all doin' okay?"

"Just fine. We came to see if I'd had any phone messages."

"Nope. Not yet. No mail, either. Say, I've got some fresh pork in the back if you need a little meat. It's real lean. Only take me a minute to cut you some nice chops."

Adam looked to Sara. "Shall we?"

"Sure. That sounds good." She patted the pocket of her jeans where she'd tucked the money from her pack. "This time, dinner's on me. You've spent enough, already."

"In that case," Adam said, winking at Farley, "How about the biggest, most expensive steak you've got?"

Shaking his head, the old man started to make his way around the counter. "Beans and corn bread's all we had when I was growin' up. Nowadays, everybody complains about plain, good food like that.

There was a flatlander by here just the other day carryin' on somethin' awful about havin' to eat cold beans right out of the can. You'd a thought he was being poisoned.''

Adam stiffened. "A flatlander?"

"Yeah. We don't get many o' them way up here. He was a nosy fella, too. Asked a lot of questions." He paused and glanced back at Sara. "Come to think of it, he mentioned the old Stone place. Maybe he's kin, too."

Instinctively, Adam slipped his arm around Sara's shoulders and felt a barely perceptible shiver as he asked, "What did you tell him?"

Farley shrugged. "Nothing much. Didn't like his looks. Kind of shifty-eyed, he was."

Adam tightened his grip. "Okay. If he comes back, you haven't seen Sara. Got that? Don't tell him a thing." Perceiving the old man's nervous reaction, Adam was afraid the warning came too late.

Temporarily suspending her reservations about getting too close to Adam, Sara leaned against him for physical and emotional support. "What did this man look like?"

"Oh, I don't know. Just a fella. Kind of tall. Brown hair. He had a funny little mustache. Looked like a caterpillar had up and died on his lip."

Adam felt her stiffen. He was afraid her knees might buckle but she surprised him by standing firm as he told the old man they'd wait on the porch until he filled their order.

Outside, Adam took her by the shoulders, guided her to a weathered old rocking chair and commanded, ''Sit.'' The fact that she followed his instructions and didn't argue worried him more than the idea that Rydell might have located her. Adam dropped to one knee in front of her, his hands on the arms of the chair. Encircling, protecting.

''I'm okay,'' she insisted.

''In a pig's eye.''

One corner of Sara's mouth lifted wryly. ''I'd rather have a pork chop.''

''That's more like it. You had me worried for a minute. This guy really has you spooked, hasn't he?''

There was a faraway look in her eyes. ''Eric started to grow a mustache just before school recessed for the summer. I thought it looked funny, too.''

''Okay. So let's assume he got this far. That doesn't mean he's still around. Maybe he gave up and went home.'' Adam tried a joke. ''Maybe the canned beans killed him.''

''That was pretty lame.'' Still, she smiled in appreciation.

''Well, I'm not as good at seeing the ridiculous side of things as you are, yet. But I'm learning.''

Her grin broadened, her heart opened. She laid a

hand gently over his and looked into his understanding gaze. "You sure are. I've never had a better student."

Following Adam's original plan, they headed for Sara's car as soon as they were finished at the store. Some of the terrain was so rough, the roadway so narrow, she wondered if they'd make it through, even in the four-wheel-drive truck.

She braced herself with one hand on the dash, the other holding on to the back of the seat, and tried to keep from bouncing around too badly. "None of these roads are marked. How do you know where we're going?"

"After you've lived up here awhile you get used to the twists and turns and just remember what's where."

"I suppose so." A frightening thought struck. "Did I drive this awful road in the storm?"

Adam shook his head. "Not this part of it. You were coming from the opposite direction. You got stuck before you came to the really bad sections."

"Thank you, God," Sara whispered, closing her eyes for an instant of pure gratitude to her Heavenly Father.

"I suppose you could see it that way. I prefer to call it luck."

"Why?" It seemed like a sensible question, given her current mood of thankfulness. "Don't you think

God cares about us? I do.'' The truth of her plain statement hit her squarely in the conscience. She *did* believe it! No matter how many times she'd doubted God's watchful eye because of her problems with Eric, the Lord was still up there. Still vigilant. Still in charge.

"I used to think He cared," Adam said flatly. "But that was a long time ago. In another life."

In his life as a cop, Sara reasoned. Of course. That made perfect sense. She'd had to deal with only one negative element in her life and she'd felt her faith fading as a result. What must it have been like for a man who faced evil every day on the job?

She wanted to say something—anything—that would change his mind, open his heart to the Lord once again. But nothing meaningful came to mind, not even when she prayed silently for the right words.

Frustrated, she prayed harder, then gave up in disgust. For her, one of the hardest parts about being a Christian was waiting patiently for God's perfect timing. Patient, she wasn't. Not even a little.

Wriggling around on the seat to see why Adam was stopping, she spotted the abandoned rental car. In the daylight, its position didn't look quite as precarious as it had during the storm.

"Oh, good—it didn't slide into the river!"

"Apparently not." Cautious, he inched the truck

closer. When Sara started to get out he said, "No. Stay here."

Puzzled, she scowled at him. "Why?"

"Because I said so."

It was his tone of voice that caused her to obey. She watched him step down, check the ground around the stranded vehicle, then glance inside. Finally, he motioned for her to join him.

"What is it? What's wrong?" She slid to the ground and made a headlong dash for the car.

Adam grasped her shoulders firmly to stop her. "He's been here."

Peering past him she said, "I don't understand. How can you tell?"

"Everything's gone."

"Everything?" Sara felt her resilience ebbing. "But, how…?"

"Looks like he walked in, loaded up with whatever he could carry, and left. The stuff he couldn't take, he tossed over the bank into the river."

"Oh, no." She searched her mind for any excuse to refute Adam's conclusions. "How do you know it was Eric? I mean, somebody else could have stumbled on the car and just helped themselves, couldn't they?"

"Not the folks who live around here," he countered. "These people take care of each other. They would never have stolen your things. They wouldn't have wasted anything useful by pitching it over a cliff, either.''

Sara was out of rationalizations. Adam was right, of course. She sighed and nodded sadly, felt his hands tighten on her shoulders. He was all she had. The only one who believed her. The only one who ever had. And she was so thankful to be with him she could hardly stand it.

Swaying, she laid her palms on his chest, her forehead resting above them. ''I really need a hug.''

Bad idea, his logical side warned. Next thing you know, she'll be wanting another kiss.

That thought was his undoing. Enfolding her in a tight embrace, Adam closed his eyes and held her, knowing he was making a terrible mistake, yet unwilling to walk away. Whatever else happened, he must remember that Sara was only there, only in his arms, because she craved his protection. Not because she held any fondness for him. And not because he cared for her on a personal level, either.

She raised her face and looked up at him with misty eyes the color of the forest at dusk. Adam tried to banish the romantic mood by making a joke and starting to release her. ''That's all. Only one hug to a customer.''

''How about your kisses?'' Sara whispered boldly. ''Are they rationed, too?'' She slid her arms around his neck, refusing to let him go. Her lips parted. ''I hope not.''

Adam could have laughed, could have grasped her wrists and loosened her grasp. He could have flown without an airplane, too, if he'd had that much willpower. He lowered his mouth to hers and surrendered, instead.

Deepening the kiss, drowning in the sensations, Sara knew she was clinging to him like a boat adrift in a hurricane. He was her anchor. Her lifeline. The answer to her prayers for deliverance, even if he did refuse to acknowledge his part in God's great plan.

In her mind and heart, there was more going on than just a simple hug and a kiss. Putting her complete trust in Adam had become an integral part of her expression of faith.

But could there be more to it than that? Was there, already? If only she wasn't so distracted by his marvelous kisses, maybe she could think clearly, decide what was really going on. The reasoning was compelling enough to bring her to her senses, cause her to break away.

Blinking rapidly, she held him at arm's length. Too much more of Adam Callahan and she was likely to forget everything else, including her vow to save herself for marriage! That would never do. She already had enough problems. Once Eric was out of her life and the danger was past, she'd let herself consider how she really felt about her protector.

And until then? Sara stared at Adam. He was

breathing as hard as she was. She'd gotten so comfortable being with him that she'd foolishly forgotten he was a normal, healthy man with the same strong urges she had. Only chances were good *he* hadn't promised anyone he'd remain celibate, let alone made a solemn vow to God.

She sobered. No matter how much she needed the comfort of Adam's strength, no matter how alone and lost she felt, she'd better remember just who and what she was dealing with.

Yes, she believed the Lord would continue to look after her, but she also knew better than to mock Him by behaving impulsively. It was one thing to swear her trust was in God and another to stand in the middle of a railroad track in front of a speeding train to prove it.

"I think we should be heading home," she finally said.

Adam agreed completely. He gestured at the car. "Don't touch anything here. We'll swing by Burnham's on the way back and tell the sheriff what's happened. Then, if we can't get a decent tow truck up here soon, I'll try to pull you out, myself."

"You?"

"Why not? You can't stay stranded forever."

He really wanted to get rid of her, didn't he? Sara thought with chagrin. Well, why not? They hardly knew each other. She shouldn't be surprised to hear that Adam hadn't been impressed by the few simple kisses they'd shared. He'd undoubtedly kissed a lot of other, more worldly women.

Besides, he was only being sensible. She was the impulsive one, the one who always assumed the best and took a chance. What a fool she'd been to imagine there could be more to their dawning relationship than there already was.

In her opinion, there was no use delaying the inevitable. "Try it now," she ordered.

"I beg your pardon?" Adam was frowning, looking confused.

"Try to pull the car out, now. You might as well. We're already here."

"If we touch it, move it, the sheriff won't be able to use it as evidence."

"Evidence for what? Vandalism? Petty theft? Give me a break. Eric's not going to pay for messing with my car and you know it."

"When you're right, you're right," Adam conceded. "Stand over there, out of the way. I'll go turn my truck around."

"Good. Fine. Just do it."

Sara made her way to the forested side of the road and stood there with her arms crossed, her mood plummeting. How could she have been so wrong about seeing God's hand in her meeting with Adam? Was she back to her old tricks of second-guessing the Lord and trying to make things happen according to her own views of divine guidance?

She supposed so. It was typical of her. She just wished she'd been right this time.

But obviously she hadn't been. Adam hadn't argued a bit when she'd suggested he free her car immediately. There was no getting around it. As soon as the stupid car was back on the road she'd lose her excuse to stay with Adam Callahan any longer and he'd be glad to be rid of her. It was as simple as that.

Chapter Seven

Sighing, Sara watched Adam back his truck up to her car and attach a heavy chain to the towing hook beneath the front bumper. Watching him work was painful. It meant their time together was almost over.

And there she stood, brooding and wasting their last few minutes, when she could be helping him, instead. Chastened, she jogged back across the road. "Can I help?"

He wiped his muddy hands on a rag from his toolbox. "Yup. Stay out of the way."

"Can't I steer or something? Put on the brakes? If my car comes loose and there's no driver, what's to keep it from hitting your truck?"

"*If* your car comes loose?"

"When. I mean, when."

"That's better." Adam sized up the situation. Sara did have a valid point. "Okay. It can't slide over the bank now that it's chained to the truck so it should be safe enough. Get in carefully so you can steer. Just keep your foot off the brake till I tell you."

"Yes, sir." She gave him a mock salute, then headed for the stranded car.

Behind her, Adam merely shook his head. The woman was indomitable. She'd probably grin even if she were on her way over Niagara Falls in a barrel. A leaky barrel.

Cautious, Sara opened the door and inched her body inside. There was already so much mud in the poor rental car she decided to forgo trying to clean her boots, first. At this point, she figured the most important task was to pay attention to Adam and do exactly as he said.

No, she didn't particularly want to be made capable of driving off into the sunset like some cowboy hero in an old western movie. She also didn't want to disappoint her benevolent companion. Adam was giving her rescue his all. She could do no less.

She stuck her hand out the window and waved. "I'm ready."

The truck eased away. Adam was sitting sideways, looking back at her. When the chain tightened, the car gave a little jerk. "No brakes," he shouted.

Sara was careful to keep her feet off all the pedals. Her hands gripped the wheel, her knuckles whitening. "Okay."

Adam gave the truck more gas. The wheels spun, then caught, spun, then caught. The little car bucked and shuddered but it was axle-deep in clay and high-centered on the berm as well. It wouldn't budge. This was *not* working out the way he'd planned.

He shut off the truck's engine and walked back to where Sara sat.

"I did exactly what you said," she insisted before he reached her. "No brakes. Honest."

"And it's in neutral, not in gear, right?" Leaning in the open window, he glanced at the shift lever.

"Neutral? Uh-oh." Sara didn't catch exactly what he said next. Which was just as well, considering the tone of his voice. "You never told me to shift any gears," she alibied.

"I never told you to get stuck in the first place and you managed quite well."

"Thanks. I did my best."

All Adam said was, "Put it in neutral," as he strode stiffly back to his truck.

She did so and waited. Once again the chain tightened. This time, though, Adam used the slack to give the car a serious jerk. It shuddered. Bucked. Slipped sideways, then came forward just far enough to drop the rear wheels into the soggy depression left by the chassis.

That was the end of the road for Sara's car. It settled into the ruts as if there were powerful suction in the bottom of each hole.

Adam continued to pull. Too late he realized that even a four-wheel-drive vehicle was not immune to getting mired, given enough mud and the right conditions. Or the *wrong* conditions, plus Sara's so-called help.

Disgusted, he left the motor idling and got out to remove the tow chain, hoping the truck could extricate itself if it wasn't trying to tow the car. The rear bumper was flush with the roadbed, which put the chain below that, completely out of sight. He started to dig for it with his hands, clawing at the soupy, clay muck. The shadow that fell across his efforts told him he had an audience. And she was giggling.

He snorted derisively. "What's so funny?"

"You are." Sara was so relieved that she wouldn't be able to drive away from him she could hardly contain her elation. "I think you're stuck."

"No way." Continuing to dig, he threw aside handsful of mud in globs.

"Want a shovel?"

"Got one?"

"No. I thought you'd have one."

"If I did, would I be doing this?" he countered, flinging a handful of red clay at her feet.

"I don't know. Would you? It looks like good

therapy. Besides it's fun. My kids love to play in clay. Most of them usually try to make dinosaurs.''

Adam glared up at her. ''Lady, if you ask me to make you a dinosaur out of this clay, I'm going to…''

''You're going to what?'' she interrupted. Bending slowly, she scooped up a small handful of the sticky, oozy red mud.

His eyes widened. ''Don't even think it.''

''Think what?'' Sara put on her most innocent-looking expression. The man was on his knees, up to his elbows in gunk, and she was on her feet, standing above him. Any way you looked at it, she had a distinct advantage.

''Sara, I don't like that look in your eyes.''

''Who, me? I didn't do anything,'' she purred. ''Yet.'' She hadn't intended to, either, until Adam's arm shot out and he grabbed her ankle. She resisted. Tried to pull away. The effort jerked her feet out from under her.

On the way down she lobbed the handful of goo at him. It wasn't a direct hit but it did splash onto his face making him look like he'd caught mud pox.

With a solid plop, she hit the ground, squealing. ''Adam! No!'' She tried to wriggle away. ''I didn't mean to get you dirty. It was just a reflex. Honest it…''

''Aargh!'' He lunged at her, both hands outstretched, fingers dripping.

Sara rolled, scrambled, almost escaped before he connected solidly with the leg of her jeans, leaving a distinct handprint. "You dirty..." She crawled the rest of the way out of arm's reach, then twisted around to inspect the damage.

"Dirty, is right," he bellowed. "You should see yourself."

"Me? Me?" Giggling uproariously, she shook her hands, flinging drops of mud right and left. "Looks like you got the worst of it."

Adam staggered to his feet and bent to rest his hands on his knees. He was laughing so hard he was breathless. "We're going to have to do laundry again."

"No kidding." She approached cautiously. "Truce?"

"Truce. I can't win with you, anyway."

"I'm glad you realize that." Sara wiped one hand on her jeans to dry it and held it out to him. "Walk me home? I could go by myself, except I have no idea which way the cabin is from here."

"I should leave you right where you stand."

"But you won't. You're the hero type. They never abandon helpless females."

Adam laughed. "Lady, you're about as helpless as a porcupine in a phone booth."

"Nice analogy. Is that a bit of local lore?"

"Nope. I adjusted it to fit you. I think the original

saying has something to do with a skunk and out-door plumbing.''

''And you changed it to a nice little porcupine just to keep from hurting my feelings.'' She made a silly face. ''Awww. I'm touched.''

His smile was lopsided and smug. ''Don't know that I'd go getting all misty-eyed if I were you. Por-cupines can be formidable if they're cornered.''

Sara sobered, nodded. ''Funny. That was how I felt till I met you. Cornered. Trapped in a situation not of my making.'' She reached out and took his hand. ''In case I haven't told you lately, I'm very grateful for all your help.''

Touched, Adam knew she meant every word. He also knew they were putting a terrible strain on their mutual self-control by remaining together in his small cabin any longer than was absolutely neces-sary. His mind churning, he cast around for another alternative. Any option that would ensure Sara's safety as well as preserve his own sanity. The more attracted he was to her, the more he realized the volatility of the situation. This was not a woman to be trifled with, nor was he the kind of man to take unfair advantage. He liked her. Truly liked her. As a person. As a friend. That was plenty, given his history. Which brought him back to the reason he'd hidden himself away in the hills, become a recluse.

''Maybe you can help me in return,'' he finally said. ''Can you think of someplace else to stay, besides with the Burnhams?'' The crestfallen look on Sara's face cut him to the quick. "I mean, it's pretty crowded in my cabin and I just thought…''

"I could camp out in your yard if you don't want me inside, I suppose,'' she said quietly. "I've really tried not to be a nuisance.'' Eyeing his muddy jeans she added, "Most of the time, anyway.''

Adam smiled to put her at ease. "It's not that. I'm just afraid your reputation will suffer by your staying with me.''

She huffed. "My reputation is between me and the Lord. Sure, I care about what other people think. Everybody does. But as long as I believe I'm doing what God wants me to do, He's really the only one I have to answer to.'' She squeezed Adam's hand. "Of course, there's *your* reputation to think of, too.''

"You're joking, right? I don't get to town except for supplies. I'm not interested in becoming a part of any community, no matter how benevolent.''

"Country people are very accepting,'' she said.

"Which is why they leave me alone and let me live the kind of life I've chosen.'' He cast a disgusted glance at his incapacitated truck. "Come on. I'll pull my keys and we'll head for home cross-country, like we did when I first found you.''

"It could be worse,'' Sara offered.

Adam didn't see how. He wasn't used to failing when he tried to do something physical, like pull her car out of the mud. Nor was he accustomed to living under the same roof with such an upbeat character. Sara's lively, sunny presence was disconcerting. She wouldn't even let him brood when he wanted to.

"Well," she said, "it could be."

"Okay. You win. How?" Adam pocketed the keys, grabbed the bag of groceries and started off into the woods.

Sara scurried to keep up. "It could be raining and dark, like before."

She had a point. "Don't you ever see the downside to things?" he asked cynically.

"Sure, I do. For instance, I wish I'd made it to granny's old place and met you as a neighbor, instead of your winding up stuck with me like this."

"A neighbor?" Adam stopped walking and stared at her. "Is the homestead close by?"

"I think so. I have a map, of sorts, in my pack. We can check it when we get back to the cabin."

"Well, why didn't you say so?!"

"Because you didn't ask, I guess. Is that a problem?"

"No, but it might be the answer to our predicament, especially if the old house is habitable."

"You mean we could go there?" She was so elated she clapped her hands. "Oh, how wonderful. I'd be willing to walk *miles* to see it, again."

"That depends on the terrain, as well as the weather. Don't get your hopes up too soon."

"It's never too soon for hope," Sara countered. "You should try it sometime."

"Hope is an emotion for fools. I'm a lot smarter than that."

"Then I'm sorry for you," she said quietly. "If you think with your head instead of your heart, you miss a lot of the blessings of life."

"You also miss the heartache," Adam countered, expecting her rebuttal.

Instead, she looked at him with empathy and said, "For once, we agree."

The map Sara had of the homestead was a topographical rendering that told Adam all he needed to know. He pointed to the tattered piece of paper. "Here's about where we are, now. See the ridge?"

She nodded. Adam was leaning over her as she sat at the table with the map spread out in front of her. His presence was so overwhelming she could barely concentrate on what he was saying. They'd taken turns showering and getting cleaned up and she could smell the tangy aroma of his aftershave. Imagine what it would be like to caress his smooth cheek with her palm. Such inclinations presented a distinct hazard to her emotional stability. Yet they kept intruding into her otherwise lucid thoughts in spite of her determination to push them aside.

He braced an arm on the table and leaned closer. His shirtsleeve was rolled up, revealing the dusting of dark brown hair on his strong forearm. When he'd emerged from the bathroom, his shoulder-length hair had been slicked back, further accentuating the latent strength in his neck and shoulders.

Sara wondered how the man could look so much better without changing a thing about himself. Clearly, she was getting more aware, more appreciative of him as an individual, as time passed.

"I think we can make the trip there and back in a day, if we get an early start," Adam said. "What do you think?" When she didn't reply, he added, "Sara?"

"Hm? Oh, sure. Whatever you say."

"That's a first," Adam teased, straightening. "Since when do you go along with my ideas so easily?"

The minute he stepped back and gave her some space she shot out of the chair and hurried across the room. She made a point to look out the window for distraction, rather than spend one more second concentrating solely on her companion's considerable attributes. "I never argue...except when you're wrong, of course."

"Of course. My mistake." He sat down on the sofa and casually propped his boots on a wooden nail keg he used for both storage and a makeshift footstool.

"See what I mean?" Sara giggled nervously. When she turned, Adam was shaking his head and smiling. His hair had dried enough that a lock of it had fallen over his forehead, begging to be smoothed back. By her. She ignored the urge. "Can we go, tomorrow?" she asked.

"If you want. I'll pack some food. We'd better be prepared in case we have to spend the night."

"Do you think we might be able to stay there? That *I* might be able to? By myself, I mean."

"I don't see why not, once we're sure the place is secure and I've heard from my friends on the force so we know there's no real danger. Judging by the footprints he left around your car, Eric's visit took place a while back. Probably the same day he asked Farley about you. I have an idea he's long gone by now."

Sara sighed with relief. "Well, why didn't you say so?"

"I just did."

"I mean before, when we were back at the car."

"You didn't ask."

"Oh, right. My error." Mulling over her deepest wishes, she added, "Does that mean you're prepared to answer all my other questions without reservations?"

"I never said that." One eyebrow raised and he studied her. "What, exactly, was it you wanted to know?"

"Lots of things," she said, managing a smile meant to put him at ease. "For starters, tell me about your life before you came here."

"I thought we were discussing my professional opinion of Rydell."

"We were. Sort of. I'd just like to know more about you. As a person. I get the feeling there's a lot more to your personality than you choose to show."

Adam dodged the query. "And you can't understand that kind of thing because you're so candid. We're just different kinds of people, that's all. Surely, your friends back home aren't all like you." He wanted to add that he was certain there could be only *one* Sara Stone, but thought better of it. The less he complimented her, the easier it would be to continue to keep her at arm's length.

Sara sobered. "My friends..." Making a wry face, she continued. "They loved Eric, bought all his lies. Even the ones about me. How could that be? I don't act like a nutcase, do I?" She waved her hands at him. "Never mind. I don't think I want to hear the answer to that."

"Yes, you do. You're not crazy," Adam assured her. "But you have to remember that a sociopath like Rydell has a distinct advantage over you or me. He's operating on the belief that, whatever he chooses to do or say, he's justified. It's like a lack of conscience. And it allows him to appear totally convincing. Average people would blush or stammer or contradict themselves. He doesn't. So, everybody tends to believe him simply because that's what our instincts tell us to do.''

"But *I* figured him out.''

"Yes, you did. After you were already involved. Standing on the outside, looking in, there's no way you'd have seen through him, either. You're too trusting."

"I'll take that as a compliment.''

"You should." So much for keeping his constructive opinions about Sara to himself. Well, at least he hadn't told her she was pretty. Beautiful, was closer, anyway. Or that her hair reminded him of butterfly wings when it touched his cheek. Or that her skin was as soft as warm satin. Suddenly restless, he shifted his position.

"Then it's only fair that I give you a compliment, too," Sara returned.

Adam waited, hoping she wouldn't say something intimate and inspire an impulsive response from him that they'd both be sorry for.

"I think you have the most wonderful…dog," she said, smiling.

Adam's jaw dropped.

Her grin widened. "What? Did you think I was going to say you're good-looking, or fun to be with, or a blessing in disguise? Well, forget it, mister." She was chuckling by now. "I don't intend to say or do anything that would make things harder for us than they already are.''

''Thanks,'' he replied, trying not to laugh.

''You're welcome. If I didn't have a personal rule against telling even one white lie, I'd also say you're a lousy kisser.''

''But that would be a lie?''

''Oh, yeah,'' Sara said, blushing. ''That would be a real whopper.''

Chapter Eight

Morning dawned clear and bright. Adam was up with the sun. Sara managed to be civil by keeping her mouth shut until she'd had two cups of strong coffee.

She was seated at the table, still struggling to wake up, when he offered her one of the corn cakes he'd been making in an iron skillet. "Here. You have to eat."

"Thanks." She accepted the small, round cake with dawning recognition. "Hey, this is—"

"A corn dodger. I learned how to make them when I first moved up here."

"I know." Sara was delighted. "Granny Stone used to make these for me, too. I didn't remember them until you handed me this one." She bit into it and closed her eyes in appreciation. "Umm. This is so good."

"Thanks."

"Hers were smaller, I think. They must have been. I used to fill my pockets with them and snack all day."

"That's kind of what I had in mind. We'll need to eat on the trail and I wanted it to be easy."

Sara looked over at him with wonder. "You're really something, you know that?"

"Who, me? What did I do?"

"You took me in, fed me, and gave me a place to stay. And now you're going out of your way to continue to help me when you could have passed me off to the sheriff, instead."

"That never occurred to me." Adam was shocked to realize he spoke the absolute truth.

"Probably because you're so sure you can do a better job of protecting me," Sara said wisely.

That had to be it. "I suppose so. I'm sure the sheriff is a busy man. No telling how much time he could devote to your problems. And we are in a pretty defensible position up here. Between Samson's guarding instincts and the isolation of the cabin, nobody'll ever sneak up on us."

"Mmm, hmm." Sara popped the last bite of corn dodger into her mouth and arose. "I'll go get my pack and you can fill it with those delicious corn meal thingees."

Adam chuckled. "They're not all for you, you know."

"Aww. Now he tells me." She patted Samson's broad head as she passed. "What about our friend, here? What's he going to eat?"

"I thought I'd let you carry his dog food, since you and he are such pals, and I'd carry the people food."

"Let him carry his own food. He eats a ton."

"Actually, that's exactly what he'll do. I have saddlebags for him."

"How cute. Like a pack mule?" Adam was full of surprises, wasn't he? What an interesting man. And he looked even more handsome this morning, she noted with chagrin. Just when she thought he couldn't get any more appealing, he did just that.

Companionable silence accompanied Sara and Adam for the better part of the morning. She was so aggravated by her inability to stop imagining what it would be like to fall in love with Adam, she decided to keep her mouth shut rather than take a chance she'd say the wrong thing. It was bad enough that *she* knew the disturbing turn her thoughts had taken. The last thing she wanted was to have him suspect how she felt.

Topping a ridge, they paused for a snack and a drink from the canteen Adam carried. He started to talk about the local flora and fauna. "The redbud trees are finished blooming. So are the dogwoods. You should see this place in the early spring. The pink and white blossoms are beautiful against the deep-green background of the evergreens. They make the forest look like a flower garden.''

She regarded his commentary with reverence. ''And then all the oaks leaf out for summer. You really do love it up here, don't you?''

''Yes.''

''It's not just the isolation that pleases you, either,'' Sara guessed. ''I think you've become attached to the place for its own sake.''

Adam hadn't thought about it quite like that. ''I hate to admit it, but you may be right. There's always something new to see. Something else to learn.'' He pointed through a gap in the trees. ''For instance, look over there. In the clearing. See the doe and her fawn?''

Sara froze in midmotion to keep from frightening the deer. ''Oh...Look at those big ears. They're adorable.''

''Lots of animals are cute. But everything out here is wild. Never forget that. The beauty of these hills can lull you into overlooking hidden dangers. There are copperheads and water moccasins, for starters. And poisonous spiders, and scorpions, and...''

''And Eric Rydell,'' Sara added, biting into a corn cake solidly. ''Until we find out differently.'' She saw Adam stiffen and scan the surrounding forest, then check to see if Samson was alerted by anything.

Sara was relieved to note that the dog had never looked more relaxed. Wide pink tongue lolling, he was staring up at her as she ate, obviously wishing she'd drop him a bite. When Adam looked away, she did.

Samson was drooling and licking his chops as Adam sat down on a nearby rock. "You're spoiling him," he said.

"Who, me?"

"Yes, you. The girl who never lies."

"I didn't lie. I just didn't volunteer information."

He got himself a corn dodger and took a bite. "Isn't that called a sin of omission, according to the Bible?"

"Beats me." She was surprised he'd brought up that kind of thing. "I've only been a Christian for a short time. There's a whole lot I don't know."

"I see."

The way he said it bothered her enough to make her add, "It's a long story."

"We've got all day."

It occurred to Sara that perhaps the Lord was giving her the perfect opportunity to witness. The trouble was, the story of her faith wasn't all that impressive. Especially not lately. Truth to tell, she'd pretty much fallen away, thanks to her problems with Eric.

Still, Adam had asked, so she began to explain. "I told you my granny took me to church for the first time. After that, I kind of drifted spiritually. You know how kids are. They live for the moment. I didn't start attending church regularly until I was grown. A friend from work took me with her and I seemed to fit in."

Sara paused, unsure of how much more she should say. A feeling of harmony with God's will urged her to continue. "One Sunday I was sitting there, the way I always did, and I suddenly felt different. Like I had to do something. When the preacher gave the invitation, I almost ran down the aisle." She smiled in fond remembrance. "I was afraid I'd be embarrassed but I wasn't. It was really a wonderful experience."

"Then what happened?" Adam's brow was furrowed, his concentration focused.

Sara found his attention a little unnerving. "I settled in, went to Sunday school and church on a regular basis. You know, the usual. Everything seemed better than ever to start with, only..."

"Only what?"

Sara was chagrined to have to admit her failings. "I guess I thought nothing else would ever go wrong in my life. But it did." She lowered her lashes, stared at her feet without seeing. "I don't know. I just seemed to lose my confidence, little by little."

Looking up again, she met Adam's direct gaze. "I know you won't understand this because you love your solitary life, but I was lonely. I prayed and prayed for the Lord to send me someone special. When Eric was hired to teach at the same school and we seemed so suited to each other, I was certain my prayers had been answered."

"Hah! Answered prayer. What a joke."

Sara was instantly sorry she'd bared so much of her past to his unfeeling scrutiny. "It's not funny."

"Sure, it is." Adam snorted derisively. "You just got smart sooner than I did, that's all. I was in church all my life before I realized I was wasting my time."

"I didn't mean *that*," Sara insisted. "I've never felt that way. It was just…"

Adam stopped her. "Never mind. It doesn't matter." He stood. "Come on. We'll never get where we're going if we sit around talking all day." He patted his leg and called, "Samson. Come."

It took Sara a few seconds to comfortably reposition her backpack and follow them. She stared at Adam's broad back while she wondered what she could do or say that might heal the deep wounds he carried in his soul. Even if she was privy to the details of whatever had caused him to renounce his faith, that didn't guarantee she'd know how to help.

But God knew. Trudging through the woods, Sara couldn't close her eyes or kneel to pray. She didn't have to. It was enough to simply let her heart call out to the Lord, to place Adam before Him, and to ask for his healing to begin.

Nothing more was possible. Nothing more was necessary.

It was almost noon when they started down a narrow path into the hollow where the Stone homestead lay. Adam hadn't said a word about how close they were getting to their goal but Sara knew as surely as if there had been signs pointing the way.

Her pulse quickened. "This is it. I know it is." She pushed past him and skidded the rest of the way to the bottom of the hill, then motioned for Adam to come, too. "Look—over there across the creek. That's where the well is. And the house is on the other side of the barn. Hurry."

With Samson galloping ahead and Adam behind, Sara jogged around the weathered old barn and stopped abruptly. Her mouth dropped open. The big, white-painted farmhouse she remembered so fondly was nothing more than a decrepit derelict, now. The porch roof sagged, the paint had peeled off in sheets, and the roof was missing half its tin. As she watched, a barn swallow swooped in the open front door and exited by a broken pane in a side window.

Sara stared. "Oh, my. What a shame."

Joining her, Adam was equally disappointed. "I guess we won't be staying here."

"It was beautiful, once," she said sadly. "Granny Stone had flowers everywhere around the house, and a big vegetable garden out back. Everything was so alive, then. Now, it's like the whole place is in mourning."

"I'm really sorry it's gone to pieces like this," Adam said. He touched her arm to urge her forward. "Come on. Let's look around. Maybe you'll find a memento you can take back with you."

Wild grasses had grown up around the rock foundation of the house. Among the weeds, Sara recognized remnants of the daffodils her great-grandmother had been so proud of. They grew in parallel rows along what had once been the front walkway, then branched out to frame the small yard like a foot-high fence.

Sara pointed to the slim leaves. "These are the first flowers of spring. Granny said daffodils'll poke up right through the snow, if there's any left on the ground when it's time for them to bloom. Let's see if we can find a shovel so we can take some bulbs back to your cabin and plant them there."

"Why?" Adam was frowning.

"To make it more homey?"

"It's fine like it is," he countered.

"You don't have to worry about them hurting the forest. They're natural. At least they used to be, a long time ago. Folks used to go out in the woods and dig them, then bring them home to brighten up their farms.''

"That's probably why you don't see them in the wild much anymore," Adam remarked. "Like ginseng. The commercial harvesters have just about decimated the stuff around here."

That was a surprise to Sara. "Ginseng? Like in the health food stores?"

"The same. It's the root they're after, so once it's dug up, the plants are history."

"What a shame." She led him closer, stepping onto the rickety porch with care, then peering in the open door. "Speaking of a shame. It looks like the old floor is ready to give out."

Adam leaned past her to look and nodded. "It sure does. I wouldn't go inside if I were you. The holes we can see are probably not the only weak points. I imagine the whole place is ready to fall down."

She would have struck a melancholy pose and leaned against the doorway if the opening hadn't been in use as a flyway for red wasps. Ducking out of the way of the irate insects, Sara abandoned the house to its resident critters and started for the barn.

"It's amazing to me that there's anything left here, considering how long the place has been abandoned," she said. "I was kidding myself when I dreamed of being able to come home. Of course nothing's the same. How could it be?" She looked up at Adam. "I suppose you think I'm impulsive for trying."

"To do what? To go back to a happier time in your life? I don't think there's anyone who hasn't wished that was possible."

"Even you?" They'd reached the cooling shadow of the barn. Adam removed his pack. Sara followed his example, placing hers on the ground next to his. It didn't surprise her that he ignored her last question.

She changed the subject. "So what do we do now?"

"Rest a bit, then head for home, I suppose. We should make better time on the way back, since we know where we're going."

"Well...maybe one of us does," she said with a smile. "Don't forget, I'm directionally challenged."

"You can always tie a string to the dog and let him lead you home."

"Right. Good idea." Sara noticed that Samson wasn't underfoot anymore. "Where did he go, anyway?"

"Beats me." Adam shouted, "Hey, Samson. Get over here."

There was no response. Not even a stirring of the tall grass behind the house.

"Maybe he's busy rounding up a flock of quail," Sara offered. "He tried to do that earlier today."

Adam shaded his eyes and scanned the distance.

"I don't know. I wouldn't worry so much about him if he wasn't wearing that pack with his food in it. If he got it caught on a fallen tree or something, it could snare him. Keep him from coming when I call."

"Then we have to find him."

"I will." Adam took off his canteen and handed it to her. "You keep this with you and wait here."

"But, I can help. Samson likes me, remember?"

"I know he does. The thing is, there are bound to be all kinds of hazards in these fields. The dog's wearing a flea collar and I've got hiking boots on to help protect me. All you've got is those rubber boots."

"Which have already given me blisters," Sara admitted. "I wish I had the sneakers I left in the car."

"They wouldn't help if you stumbled into a bunch of ticks or chiggers."

"Oooh. I remember those from when I was here, before. I'll bet I scratched for a month." The memory started the itching all over again, if only in her mind. It was enough to convince her of the folly of argument. "Okay. You go chase Samson and I'll wait here."

"Good."

"You will come back, won't you?" The question began as a wisecrack but by the time she'd spoken it, it had taken on a serious sound.

"Of course I will," Adam promised. No matter

how courageous Sara acted, there was a part of her that was afraid of being left alone. He realized that. The safest place for her, however, was right where she stood. "I don't want to have to worry about you *and* my dog," he explained. "Eat a corn dodger and have a swig out of the canteen to wash it down while you wait. Just save enough for me. We'll feed the dog and water him out of the creek when I find him."

"Okay."

Sara watched Adam walk away, pausing to search occasional patches of bare ground as he went. They'd seen the tracks of deer, raccoon and wild turkeys on their trek to the old homestead. Surely, Samson's enormous paw prints would stand out enough that Adam could trail him, once he decided which direction he'd gone.

Sara's glance wandered over the ground at her feet even though she knew the effort was futile. Samson hadn't been with them when they'd walked to the barn so his tracks wouldn't be there. Still, looking gave her something with which to occupy her mind.

Most of the yard around her had dried on the surface. One muddy depression remained where the sagging barn door had worn away the soil from years of being opened and closed. In that depression, Sara spotted a distinct footprint.

It was human.

Chapter Nine

Sara gasped. Her first instinct was to scream. Fortunately, before she gave vent to her fright, her brain registered the fact that the print was small, about the size one of her students might have made if he'd been barefoot.

She bent down to get a better look at the faint tracks. Out of the corner of her eye she saw a shadow move inside the barn. Pretending to be unaware she wasn't alone, she tugged the wooden door open farther, then stepped through.

The place smelled musty. Dust motes danced and twinkled in the sunbeams shining through the gaps in the high roof. Mice scuttled for cover.

Fond memories tugged at the edges of Sara's consciousness. There used to be a soft-eyed, brown cow tethered in an end stall for milking twice a day. And there'd also been an old, grey-nosed mule whose broad back she'd climbed onto whenever she got the chance, pretending she was actually astride a beautiful pony.

She smiled. How simple and lovely her childhood had been during that one, perfect summer. And speaking of children... Her eyes fell on a series of miniature tracks leading to the foot of the ladder to the loft.

Made of narrow crosspieces nailed to rough timbers for uprights, the ladder hadn't been particularly sturdy in its heyday. By now, it looked anything but safe. Rather than climb it, she decided to call out, "You can come down, now. I'm friendly."

Sara heard a rustling above her. There was somebody up there all right. Someone small. "I'll bet you're about six years old, aren't you? Maybe seven? It's really hard to tell from way down here."

Still, no child appeared. Could she have been mistaken? After all, she wasn't a native tracker. Maybe the footprints had been made long ago. Except that recent rains would have obliterated the track by the door if that were the case.

She decided to use psychology. Picking up a stick, she began to scratch letters in the dirt floor. "My name is Sara," she wrote in large, block letters. Then she added, "My great granny Stone lived here."

Movement in the loft proceeded to the end of the

barn. As Sara watched, a small, bare foot showed on the top rung of the ladder. Then another. She held her breath, worried about frightening her diminutive companion.

Sagging jeans came next, followed by a T-shirt that hung almost to his knees, and a mop of reddish-brown hair. The little boy was not unusually thin, she decided. It was his oversize clothes which made him seem frail. She smiled broadly as he peered at her over his shoulder and cautiously worked his way down to ground level.

Sara greeted him with a cordial, "Hi."

The child nodded shyly.

"What's your name?"

"Bobby Joe." He spoke so quietly she could barely hear him.

"I'm Sara," she said. "But I guess you already know that, huh?"

"No, ma'am."

She stepped back and pointed to the floor. "I mean, I wrote it for you. Here. I thought you could see it from where you were hiding."

Bobby stared at the dirt at his own feet and shook his head, refusing to look at the letters she'd made.

It occurred to Sara that he was acting as if he couldn't read. Of course, his reticence could be because he was shy. Or worried about being caught trespassing. It could also be because he wasn't keen on formal education and wanted nothing to do with proving his skills.

"What grade are you in?" she asked.

He looked up, apparently surprised by her question. "Second."

"At the school where I come from, I teach kindergarten and first grade," she explained. When the little boy's eyes widened and he looked at her as if she'd suddenly grown two heads, she laughed. "It's okay, Bobby. I'm on vacation."

"Whew." He chanced a grin of relief. "Good."

"Don't you like school?"

"No, ma'am. I surely don't."

"That's too bad. I think it's kind of fun." She laughed at his astonished expression. "Well, I do. I always did, even when I was little."

"That's 'cause you're a girl," he ventured, rapidly gaining courage. "My sisters like it, too."

"Do they? How many sisters do you have?"

"Two. Brenda's ten and Rhonda's twelve. We live with Mamaw Mullins."

"Your grandmother?" Sara found the parallel with her own young life interesting. "My granny Stone used to live right here on this farm. She was actually my great-grandmother. I came here to visit her when I was just about your age."

"No kidding?"

"No kidding," Sara said, returning his broad grin.

"I'll bet I could show you where I used to have a swing tied to an old oak tree."

"It was a tire." His eyes sparkled.

She found Bobby Joe's eagerness enchanting. It reminded her why she'd become a teacher in the first place. "How did you get so smart?"

"I ain't smart," he countered. "I just saw the place." He gestured. "It's over there, by the spring."

Was it? She really didn't remember that well. "You could be right." Holding out her hand to him she asked, "Would you show me?"

"Sure. Come on." With the natural trust of a young child, he placed his smaller hand in hers and led her out of the barn.

They made their way across the yard to where a shallow creek flowed over flat ledges of shale in a rippling cascade. Tadpoles darted for cover when the shadows of woman and child fell on the water.

"You won't get chiggers if you go through that long grass barefoot, will you?" Sara asked, concerned that he might not act sensibly if he was showing off for her.

"Naw." The boy pointed. "See the little yellow flowers over there?"

"The ones that look like tiny daisies?"

"Uh-huh. That's chigger weed. If we don't brush up against 'em, we'll be fine."

Sara was impressed with his indigenous expertise.

"Wow. I'm glad you told me. I guess I have a lot to learn about living here, don't I?"

"Guess so."

"Maybe you could teach me?"

"I 'spose."

"Good. And to make it fair, I'll let you play with my laptop computer. I don't have it with me right now, but I'm sure we'll meet again."

"Prob'ly will. I don't live far."

Although the boy didn't express overt enthusiasm for the chance to use the computer, Sara knew he'd love it once he had an opportunity to see what it could do. If he was a visual learner, the method was perfect for polishing his reading skills. If his tendencies were more auditory, she'd merely read aloud over his shoulder to augment whatever he was seeing on the screen.

It thrilled her to think of teaching again, even in an unofficial capacity. "Speaking of where people live, do you know a man named Adam Callahan?"

"You mean the fella you came with?"

"Yes. His place is over..." She started to point, then realized she had no idea which direction to indicate.

"Past Burnham's," the boy said. "I know. It's a ways."

"No kidding." Sara suddenly realized how weary she was. Not only had their trek been a long, tiring one, her feet hurt from where the boots had rubbed. And she was hungry, besides.

She was about to offer to share one of her corn dodgers with the boy when she remembered she'd left her pack back at the barn. That reminded her of Samson's disappearance. "You haven't seen where our big white dog went, have you?"

"Chasin' squirrels. He'll never catch 'em, though. He's too slow. Takes a mountain feist to do that."

"A what?"

Bobby Joe looked up at her as if she were dumber than dirt. "It's a huntin' dog."

"Oh. Well, I told you I had a lot to learn."

Sara glanced back toward the barn and discovered she couldn't see it from where they stood, which meant she wasn't visible, either. If Adam returned with Samson and found her missing, he'd worry unnecessarily. It was enough that he'd been looking out for her where Eric was concerned. She certainly didn't want to cause him any extra anxiety.

"How much farther to the old swing?" she asked.

"Right over here." Bobby pointed to the spot. "The tire fell down but it's still there. See?"

"That tree looks a lot bigger than it did when I was a girl," Sara remarked, shading her eyes to peer into the topmost branches where a reddish-colored fox squirrel sat scolding them.

"That's 'cause it was a long, long, *long* time ago," Bobby said wisely.

"Well, it wasn't *that* long." Smiling, she faced him, hands on her hips. "How old do you think I am?"

He scrunched his face into a thinking pose, his green eyes all-knowing. "Oh, I dunno. Maybe fifty."

"Fifty!"

The boy broke into giggles. "That's what my mamaw does when I guess her age, too."

Sara reached out and ruffled his hair. "You little stinker. You really had me fooled." She bent down to whisper, "I'm really twenty-five."

His rosy cheeks warmed with a blush. "That's what mamaw always says, too."

Adam found Samson circling an enormous white oak and acting as if he'd treed a dozen prize squirrels.

Trying to sound gruff, he said, "You're supposed to chase sheep, you mangy mutt. In case nobody ever told you, they don't climb trees."

The dog just sat there, exhausted and panting, looking terribly pleased with himself.

"I know. You can tell how glad I am to find you, so you're not worried. You're not a bit sorry, either. Are you?" He undid the buckles on the dog's saddlebags and slipped them off his back. "Come on. I'll carry this till you eat some of it and lighten the load. Let's go."

When the dog didn't respond, Adam's voice became modulated like that of a cajoling parent. "Samson, Sara's waiting. You want to go see *Sara*?"

At the sound of her name, the dog jumped up and wriggled all over with excitement.

"Yeah, I know," Adam said, half grumbling, "she affects me that way, too."

He led the way back toward the barn, keeping his eye on Samson as the dog repeatedly made unnecessary side trips into the tall grass of the abandoned pasture.

Thoughts jumbled, Adam realized he'd spoken the truth. Being around Sara did unnerve him. It was bad enough that he kept getting caught up in their shared daily concerns and forgetting that she'd be leaving the Ozarks as soon as she possibly could. Worse, there were even times when he found himself entertaining thoughts of asking her to *stay*.

Adam shook his head in disgust. What was the matter with him? Didn't he have a lick of sense, anymore? The last thing he needed was a permanent companion.

"And besides, knowing her, she wouldn't be satisfied to just hang around and keep me company like you do, would she, boy?"

Samson gamboled up, his tongue hanging out, his mouth open in a doggy smile.

"That's right. Make fun of me. See if I care."

Sobering, Adam considered the situation logically. Point one, there was no way he was going to permit Sara to leave his care until he was certain she was no longer in danger. Two, he was going to have to make sure he never touched her again, let alone was fool enough to kiss her. And three, he had to show her that he'd have done the same thing for anyone who was in trouble, so she didn't imagine that he had an inordinate interest in her.

In theory, the plan was sound. In practice, however, he had the wit and resilience of Sara Stone to cope with. Not to mention her perceptiveness with regard to his emotional status. Thank *God* the weather was still holding.

''That's not a prayer,'' he insisted, casting a jaundiced eye to the sky. ''So forget I even thought it.''

Samson barked, jolting him from his reverie. The dog had stopped in front of the barn and was nosing Sara's pack.

Adam jogged the rest of the way. ''Stop that, you glutton. You get dog food, remember?'' He paused, frowning at the abandoned backpacks. ''Sara?''

There was no answer. Adrenaline pumped. His heart threatened to beat its way out of his chest. ''Sara? Where are you?''

He'd told her to stay right there. Why wasn't she waiting for him? Surely she wouldn't have merely wandered off. Could Rydell have followed them? The odds of that were slim to none. But what other reason could there be for her to have disobeyed his orders?

Who says Sara needs a reason for anything? he thought. A sensible woman wouldn't have gotten into this mess in the first place.

Adam huffed in disgust, trying to convince himself nothing was really wrong. He scanned the ground. Saw the waffle-soled prints of her boots. She *had* walked away. After all they'd been through, after all the trouble he'd gone to in order to safeguard her, she'd disregarded his instructions and gone for a stroll around the old homestead. Just like that. Never mind the snakes or the vermin or all the other hazards he'd warned her about.

Furious, Adam cupped his hands around his mouth, took a deep breath, and shouted, "Sara!" as loud as he could.

Sara heard Adam's deep voice echoing off the surrounding hills. "Uh-oh. I think we're in trouble, Bobby Joe."

The boy agreed. "Sounds like it."

"I think we'd better get back to the barn." She held out her hand to him, saw him hesitate. "You're coming with me, aren't you?"

"I dunno. He sounds awful mad."

"A fine friend you turned out to be. Don't you dare run off on me just when I need you."

"Yes, ma'am. I mean, no, ma'am."

She laughed gaily. "Adam is really going to be surprised when he sees you."

"He's not as mean as he sounds, is he?"

"No. Not at all. Mostly, I think he's just lonesome."

"Y'all could come home with me. Mamaw always has plenty of food for company."

Sara was touched. "Thanks for the invitation. We hadn't planned to stay that long, though. If we don't start back soon I'm afraid we'll be walking in the dark and I don't want to chance that. I get lost enough when I can *see* where I'm going."

Together, she and Bobby Joe crossed the shallow creek hand in hand and stepped into the open area leading to the barn. Adam waited next to the packs, his hands on his hips, his feet planted firmly apart in a defensive stance. He looked mad enough to throttle her.

She waved her free hand and smiled, intending to disarm him by sheer charm. "Hi. I'm back."

"Wonderful." Adam was glaring at the boy. "Who's that?"

Continuing to project an amiable image, she said, "I'd like you to meet Bobby Joe. Bobby, this is Mr. Callahan." Sara cupped her hand beside her mouth and directed a stage whisper at Adam, "I told him you weren't as mean as you sounded."

"I'm not. I'm far worse," Adam countered. He knew he was overreacting but his gut was still in a knot and his heart hadn't yet slowed to anything like a normal pace. What was the matter with him, anyway? If he didn't know better, he'd think he was getting way too attached to Sara Stone.

The anxious look on the child's face as he held tight to Sara's hand tempered his anger. "But I'm not mad at you, Bobby. It's that lady you're with who drives me crazy."

Adam was relieved to see the boy relax and grin up at Sara like a coconspirator. "You're right. He ain't so bad."

The picture of Sara and the child together touched Adam's heart. She was the perfect image of a mother, caring for her son; a treasured teacher leading a student to a love of knowledge. He supposed, at Bobby's age, there wasn't all that much difference in the two.

"Bobby Joe has invited us to his house," Sara said. "I told him we couldn't go because we had to get back home, but I really would like to meet his family."

Adam crouched down to be on the same level as the boy. "What's your last name, son?"

"Poole. But my mamaw's a Mullins."

"I'm afraid I haven't lived here long enough to tell where you come from by that alone," Adam told him. "Is your house nearby?"

"Pretty close."

"Could we get there in less than half an hour?"

Bobby sized him up carefully, then nodded as if he'd passed muster. "Sure."

"Then we have time to visit." Adam straightened. "Do you think it would be all right to take my dog along? I don't want to cause problems if you have other dogs at your place."

"My papaw's got a couple a huntin' dogs. He keeps 'em penned up." Bobby approached the panting behemoth without fear and patted his head. "He's a big one, all right. Bet he eats a ton. What's his name?"

"Samson. And you're right about how much he can eat. I'll feed him and water him, then we'll go. As long as we're back here in an hour or so, that should give us plenty of time to get home before dark."

Sara caught his eye and mouthed, "Thank you."

Still in a snit, Adam merely scowled back at her, picked up the dog food, and led Samson away toward the creek.

"I'll bet he named his dog after the strong man in the Bible," Bobby ventured.

"You're right. I hadn't thought much about it, but I'll bet he did." Sara sighed, watching Adam in the distance. How long ago had he chosen the biblical name? she wondered. Was it before he'd renounced his faith? Had Jean, the woman Adam had mentioned, been his Delilah? Was that why he'd turned away from the Lord so completely? So radically?

Bobby tugged at her hand. "You look sad."

"I was just thinking."

"About him?"

Sara nodded. "Uh-huh."

"You like him. I can tell."

"Yes, I do," she admitted with a wistful smile.

"You gonna marry up with him?"

Bobby's question was so matter-of-fact it took her a moment to recognize how ridiculous it actually was. "No. Of course not. We're just sort of friends."

"Oh? Then how come you're so sad?"

The boy had a point. It wasn't sensible to feel so emotionally involved with someone she'd only met a few days before. Yet she was, wasn't she? "To tell the truth, I'm worried about him."

"Is he sick?"

"No. He's just very unhappy."

"Prob'ly needs Jesus," the boy said earnestly and without reservation. "Mamaw says that'd solve most folks' problems."

Sara gave his thin shoulders a brief hug and smiled down at him. "You have a very smart grandmother."

Bobby returned her grin. "She says that all the time, too."

Chapter Ten

Sara had imagined all kinds of different home situations for Bobby, most of which were based on a combination of her own childhood memories of the Ozarks and Hollywood's interpretation of backwoods hillbillies. Nothing could have been further from the truth.

The boy led his adult guests to a modest, one-story home perched on a knoll. Beside it was a three-sided shed in which a car and a tractor sat. Fifty-foot-high walnut trees shaded the yard and cattle grazed nearby, keeping the coarse grass in the surrounding pasture neat.

"What a pretty place," Sara remarked.

"Thanks." Bobby ran to the porch and burst in the door, yelling for his grandmother, while Sara and Adam waited outside. In moments, the slim, middle-aged woman appeared on the porch. Her hair was the same color as the boy's.

She dried her hands and smiled a greeting. "Hello. I'm Louise Mullins. Folks call me Lou."

"I'm Sara Stone, and this is Adam Callahan."

"Pleased to meet you," Lou said. "Come on in. Dinner's ready. I was just waitin' for Bobby Joe to get home to set it on the table."

"Oh, we didn't come to eat," Sara insisted. "Bobby just wanted us to meet you and his sisters."

"The girls are down to cheerleader practice at school. And my husband's taken some cattle to the sale barn." She shook their hands as her unexpected guests climbed the porch steps. "But you're more than welcome to visit with me."

Adam ordered Samson to remain outside, then caught Sara's eye with a grave nod as Lou led the way into the house. Sara understood. It was an affront to refuse to sit and have a neighborly visit when the opportunity arose. To beg off and leave now would be an insult to Bobby's grandmother.

Country manners also dictated they stay and eat when a meal was offered. After a day of living almost exclusively on corn dodgers, Sara was more than ready for something a little more substantial. "We don't mean to impose."

"Nonsense. Food's all cooked." Lou gestured toward an oak dining room table.

"Sit by me, Miss Sara," Bobby pleaded, scooting

past her and into his own place as his grandmother loaded the center of the table with heaping bowls of fried potatoes, corn and beans, and a platter of hot, chicken-fried steak.

Sara looked to Lou. "I'd like to wash my hands first."

"Of course. Where's my manners? It's through there. On the left," the older woman said. "Bobby, did you wash up, too?"

"Yes, ma'am." He displayed clean palms.

"Let's see the backs of those hands."

"Aw, Mamaw…"

Lou didn't have to say any more. The boy slid from his seat and marched past Adam, mumbling, "*He* didn't wash up, either."

Adam stifled a grin. What a little pistol. Reminded him of Gene, when he was about that age. Anything to pass the buck and get others involved in whatever trouble had come down on his head. There'd been almost ten years between him and his younger brother, which meant, as the older son, he'd been unfairly held responsible for a lot of the messes Gene had gotten himself into.

Except for the *last* one, Adam corrected. That one was solely his fault. And Gene had paid the ultimate price.

Sobering, he followed Bobby down the hall and waited his turn to use the bathroom. It had been literally days since he'd thought of Gene, which was a miracle in itself. Usually, hardly an hour went by that he didn't feel at least a twinge of the guilt he'd carried ever since his brother's untimely death.

If only God had answered my prayers, Adam thought absently. Then he came to his senses. God couldn't answer prayer unless He was real. Unless He cared about believers. Of all the prayers Adam had ever prayed, none was as important as the one meant to save Gene's life.

And that one had been ignored.

Sara left the bathroom and ran straight into Adam. The hallway was so narrow she had to sidle past him, making her notice how much bigger and more imposing he seemed in those close confines. Athletic strength radiated from him, warming her the way the sun warmed the earth after a cold winter. Rather than admit what was really on her mind she said, "Sorry about the delay. Staying for dinner, I mean."

"Can't be helped." He glanced down at Bobby. "Go on in, kid. You first."

Listening to the boy's muttering as he passed and slammed the bathroom door made Sara smile. "That one's going to be a challenge."

"How so?"

She hadn't intended to tarry in the hall in such close proximity to Adam. However, his question did deserve an answer and they couldn't very well discuss her suspicions in front of the boy or his family. At least not until Sara had proved her hunch.

Lowering her voice, she whispered, ''I don't think he reads very well, if at all. I intend to teach him.''

''When?''

''While I'm in the neighborhood. I thought I'd use my laptop and come up with some simple games he and I could play. You know. Easy stuff.''

''You're serious?''

''Of course I am.''

''Has it occurred to you that we live hours from here?''

Blushing, she looked up at Adam, waiting for him to realize what he'd said and correct the statement. He didn't.

Therefore, Sara did. ''*You* live hours from here. I don't live in Arkansas at all. Remember?''

''You know what I meant.''

''I know what it sounded like.''

Leaning back against the wall, Adam folded his arms across his chest and struck a nonchalant pose. ''Oh? And what would that be?''

His blasé attitude infuriated her. Standing tall and lifting her chin stubbornly, she said, ''It sounded like you'd forgotten that I'm only here because of an accident. We don't belong together.''

''You're right. We don't.''

Sara had hoped to hear Adam refute her claim. Instead, he'd agreed with the premise so readily her feelings were badly bruised. She knew it wasn't sensible to wish their idyllic days could continue indefinitely, yet she did. Her heart wouldn't let her do otherwise.

Too bad it's all one-sided, she mused. But at least I'm smart enough to know when somebody's not interested. Unlike Eric Rydell. Poor Eric had been too unbalanced to see the difference between his own romantic obsession and genuine shared affection. Sara saw herself as a lot smarter than that, but now she had a better idea how lost and miserable Eric had felt when she'd told him there could never be anything serious between them.

"Good thing for you I'm able to accept that," she told Adam.

"Yeah," he said flatly. "It's a good thing for you that I am, too."

Lou seated herself last, taking the chair between her grandson and Adam. Sara sat on Adam's immediate left. Not having been raised in a Christian home, she was a little taken aback when Lou reached for Bobby's hand and prepared to give thanks for their meal. There were many habits which became ingrained at an early age, weren't there? Good habits. Practices that brought a person closer to God on a daily basis and made worship easier as an adult.

Ashamed that she'd not been aware at the outset

that Lou wanted to say grace, Sara took the boy's other hand and held out her free hand to Adam. He hesitated, then accepted it, bowing his head like the others. Sara cherished the warm strength of his grip, the intimacy of his touch.

It didn't escape her that this was the first time they'd prayed together. She hoped it wasn't the last. There was something very special about going before the Father with unified thoughts and desires.

Would Adam's most private thoughts ever mirror hers? she wondered. Did he know how she treasured his touch, his mere presence? Probably not. Which was just as well, considering his avowed disinterest in her.

To Sara's shame, she didn't remember much of what Lou had said, once the blessing was over. All she knew was that Adam was holding her hand, gently yet firmly. As he released it, he gave her fingers a barely perceptible squeeze. The innocent gesture, coming so soon after his adamant denial of any romantic sentiment, was enough to bring a brief rush of tears to Sara's eyes.

Lou spent the next hour and a half regaling her guests with tales of growing up in the Ozarks. By the time the meal was over, Sara felt as if she'd known Bobby's grandmother for years.

"I'd hoped I'd be able to spend my vacation at the old homestead I told you about," Sara said.

"But from the looks of the place, it's not habitable."

"Don't doubt that. Nobody's lived over there for as long as I can remember. Probably even longer than that." Laughing lightly, she eyed her grandson. "Bobby Joe will tell you I've lived a grand long time. To listen to him, you'd think I saw the War Between the States with my own two eyes."

"I know." Sara grinned broadly. "He pegged my age at about fifty."

"Sounds like something he'd do." She gave the boy a loving glance. "His mama was just like him."

Assuming the woman had died, Sara waited politely for further explanation. She was surprised when Lou said, "We expect her home in a week or so. She travels for the rice growers co-op over by Marked Tree. I think she went all the way to China, this time, but I'm not sure. Can't keep up with her."

"Oh, I thought…"

Lou understood. "Nope. Bobby Joe's daddy's passed on. Had an auto accident. But June, that's his mama, she's just fine."

"And the children stay with you while she's gone?"

Lou shook her head, made a face. "They're here *all* the time. June sleeps on the Hide-A-Bed in the living room when she's home, which isn't all that often." Getting to her feet, she began to clear the table.

Sara jumped up to help. She'd slipped her boots off under the table and stumbled over them. "Oops. Mind if I give you a hand in my stocking feet?"

"Honey, this is Arkansas," Lou said with a chuckle. "If folks can't be themselves here, they can't do it anywhere." She eyed Adam as Bobby led him off to see his papaw's hunting dogs. Waiting until the door closed behind them, she asked, "So, where'd you light when you saw the old farm was in such bad shape?"

"It's a long story," Sara alibied. It had been clear from the older woman's dinner conversation that she wouldn't approve of cohabitation without the benefit of marriage. Sara didn't either, under normal circumstances. She was having a hard time justifying staying with Adam, even though she still believed the Lord was behind their odd alliance.

Deciding it would take too long to explain fully, she merely said, "My car got stranded near Adam's place and he took me in."

"I see. Well, I suppose it's possible to stay awhile with a handsome man like that and not get carried away," Lou drawled.

"Of course it is." Sara was relieved that the older woman accepted her innocent behavior, in spite of what it looked like on the surface.

But Lou wasn't quite finished. "I had a maiden aunt who never had a bit of trouble with men getting out of line. 'Course, she had a full beard and her eyes were crossed something awful, poor thing.''

"Are you serious?" Sara's jaw dropped.

"Nope. Just makin' a point." Chuckling to herself, she started scraping and stacking the dishes.

"Point made," Sara said. "Only there's a lot more to the whole problem than I've told you. I really can't do anything else, right now. As soon as my car's towed into town and checked for safety, I suppose I'll leave the Ozarks for good."

"Do you want to?"

"I beg your pardon?"

She shrugged. "Just asking. I was watching you and Mr. Callahan. You make a nice couple. It seems a shame to run off when he's so taken with you."

"He doesn't even *like* me."

"Oh, honey," Lou said, grinning, "have you got a lot to learn about men."

It was late afternoon by the time Sara and Adam bid the Mullins family a final goodbye. Brenda and Rhonda had finally arrived home, which meant more introductions, more excitement, and a longer period of parting. All in all, Sara was exhausted from worrying about her promise to Adam that they wouldn't tarry long.

His long strides carried him down the road rapidly. She hurried to catch up. "Hey, wait for me."

"We have a lot of time to make up."

"I know. And I'm sorry. I just didn't know how to get away sooner without hurting everybody's feelings." Panting, she tried to jog in the rubber boots and gave it up as impossible. "If you hadn't been so stubborn, we could have spent the night with Bobby's family, like they asked us to."

"You sure have a short memory."

Sara was confused. "What are you talking about?"

"Your stalker. You didn't go to stay at Burnhams' because of Rydell. The way I see it, being at Bobby's house for very long is even worse. Especially the way gossip travels up here."

"Of course," Sara said, sobered by the thought she might have inadvertently put the children in danger. "Oh, dear. I honestly didn't think of it that way. I'm glad you're more aware of what to do about all this than I am."

"I'm just using my head. If you want to see the boy again, to teach him or whatever, he should come to my place. That way, I can watch out for him better."

"But you don't have a phone. How will we tell him that's what we've decided?"

"As a matter of fact, I've already invited him to drop by. He says his grandpa can drive him up as far as Burnham's and he can walk the rest of the way in."

"Maybe it isn't safe to do that, either."

"Why not? He's eight going on forty, and he's used to tramping all over these hills. He'll do just fine."

"It's not that. I just don't want to put Bobby Joe at more risk because of Eric."

"You can't seal yourself in a little box and withdraw from the world just because of one man's obsession," Adam countered. "I should hear from my friends on the force soon. That'll give us a better idea of where we stand. If Rydell has no history of problems—and I suspect that's what we'll find out—then I don't think you'll need to worry anymore."

"Speaking of which, let's stop at the store on the way home and check for messages again. I'll feel much better once I've heard, even if the news is bad."

"I can understand that. But it'll take us too long to go that roundabout way on foot. We'll check tomorrow." Adam's pace slackened slightly. "It'll be all right, Sara."

"How can you be so sure?"

"Because I'll make it okay for you."

"How? Sometimes I feel like I'll have this black cloud hanging over me for the rest of my life."

His blue eyes darkened to the color of a stormy sky. "No, you won't."

Sara was taken aback by the sudden inflection of ruthlessness in Adam's voice. He sounded almost savage! That was a side of his personality that was new to her. She didn't like knowing that she was the one who'd brought it out.

"I'm sorry. I didn't intend to pile all my burdens on your shoulders. I'll be fine. I'm not worried."

"Knock it off," Adam said. "You don't fool me."

"I don't know what you're talking about."

"Tsk-tsk. Lying's a sin. You should know that."

"So is dumping on your friends." She managed a smile. "At least, if it isn't, it should be."

"I was about to ask you where in the Bible you found that little bit of wisdom. It didn't sound like anything I'd ever heard before."

"I think it has something to do with trusting in God, instead of man. Not that I don't trust *you*," she added quickly. "I already told you, I believe I landed in your neck of the woods for a reason."

"And I told *you*, I'm not your guardian angel."

"You could be wrong about that."

"I'm rarely wrong."

"Spoken like a man."

"Countered like a stubborn woman."

Sara began to grin. "Well, at least you noticed."

"Noticed what?" Adam led the way into the woods and began to break trail once again.

"That I'm a woman. I was beginning to wonder if my wearing this sweatshirt and these ugly rubber boots had destroyed my feminine image."

"Not hardly." He tossed the telling comment back over his shoulder. "There's no doubt in my mind that you're female."

"Really?" A different kind of awareness had crept into his speech. His voice sent tingling sensations zinging along her spine and prickled the hairs on the back of her neck. Her heart fluttered. Perhaps she'd goaded him too much for her own good. It was possible. She hadn't known Adam long enough to tell for sure whether or not he was serious.

The safest thing to do was to assume he'd meant every word about his awareness of her femininity. Rather than leave their current, emotionally charged topic alone and let Adam dwell on it as they walked, she decided to interject humor to lighten the mood. Lou's description of her fictional aunt provided the perfect inspiration.

"I'll bet you wouldn't say that if I had a beard."

"What?" He came to such an abrupt halt, Sara crashed into his broad back before she could stop.

She started to giggle at the funny look on his face when he turned to stare at her. "Or if my eyes were crossed," she added, trying to emulate the condition the way some of her students did when they were kidding around.

"What on earth are you babbling about?"

Sara raised her eyebrows dramatically. "Well... there was this maiden aunt that Lou was telling me about. Apparently, the poor woman didn't have a lot of trouble keeping men at bay. See, she had this full beard and..."

"I get the picture." Adam eyed her up and down. "Are you worried I won't be able to resist you?"

Actually, I'm more worried that you will, Sara told herself before she had time to censor her thoughts. "Lou did sort of caution me about it," she said. "I tried to explain to her that you and I were just sharing your cabin out of necessity."

"I told you your reputation around here would suffer if the word got out."

"Does it matter?" She searched his face for any sign he'd changed his mind about her, wanted her to stay the way Lou had suggested he might. "Will it matter?"

Adam turned away abruptly. "No," he said flatly. "No, it won't."

Chapter Eleven

The sun was still up but masked by the forest shadows as they made their way home. Now and then, Sara got a glimpse of a ray of welcome light that lifted her spirits. The rest of the time, she slogged along behind Adam as best she could and prayed they'd get to his cabin before her waning stamina gave out.

She didn't know when she'd been so tired. So sore. Not only were her blistered feet killing her, she'd had to overuse her leg muscles in order to walk in the boots, leading to even greater fatigue. It wasn't her nature to complain but she couldn't help lagging behind.

Finally, Adam noticed she wasn't following as closely as she had been. He turned and called, "Are you okay?"

"Oh, sure. I always crawl the last few miles home. It takes the wear and tear off my feet."

"It's hard on your knees, though." Chuckling, he waited for her to catch up. "You should have said something."

"What?"

"I don't know. Something."

"How about, 'carry me?' "

"That wasn't exactly what I had in mind."

"Okay. Let's see." Index finger on her temple, she struck the pose of a thinker. "Call me a cab?"

"You're a cab." He chuckled at her frazzled, disgusted expression. "Hey, don't look at me like that. That old joke was your idea. Remember the bit about the tow truck?"

"I remember." What surprised her was that *he* remembered.

"Would you like to sit down and rest awhile?" Adam cast around for a comfortable spot that wouldn't harbor too many forest denizens of the insect variety.

"If I sit, I may never get up again," Sara said. "You'll have to bring back a blanket from the cabin so I can spend the night right where I land."

"Are you really feeling that bad? I never know with you."

"You're not the only one. I'm hardly ever sure if I'm serious, either, and I'm on the inside, looking out."

"Terrific. Okay, here's what we'll do. I'll find you a safe spot to crash, cover you with piles of dry leaves to keep you warm, then come back for you in the morning. How does that sound?" The astounded look she gave him made him roar with laughter.

"That wasn't funny."

Adam fought to catch his breath and contain his high humor. "I thought it was. You should have seen your face. Piles of leaves. Oh, brother."

If Sara hadn't been so tired she'd have found it easier to share his good mood. She sighed. "Actually, I'm seriously considering taking you up on your offer and crashing into a heap right where I stand."

"Okay. You win. We'll take a break. I doubt we'll make it home before dark, anyway."

That was a news bulletin worthy of note. "We won't?"

"Probably not. Especially if you're as worn-out as you look."

She brushed her hair out of her eyes, her hand leaden. "That bad, huh?" As the long day and her fatigue caught up with her, tears misted her vision. "I'm sorry I'm so slow. I thought I was in pretty good shape till I met you. Don't you ever get tired?"

Adam thought it best to simply skirt the subject rather than admit to the added adrenaline rush he got every time he thought of Sara. "I'm just used to hiking, that's all." He put Samson's empty pack on the ground for her and held out his hand. "Here. Sit down on this."

"Why should I? Are you going to go get the leaves to bury me, now?"

"Yeah." Seeing her misty eyes and hearing the catch in her voice gave him a twist in the gut. Clearly, he'd pushed her too far.

Penitent, he helped her to the ground next to a broad-based oak and sat beside her. Slipping one arm around her shoulders he gently pulled her closer, cradling her against his chest. "Just relax. Take it easy."

Sara knew she should object. And she would, too. In a minute. But just for a little while she wanted to let herself rest as Adam had suggested. Surely, it couldn't hurt to lean against him, to rest her cheek on his warm, comforting chest and close her eyes for a few moments. It felt so good, so right, to be in his arms—even with no romance involved. There was a perfection to their being together that transcended earthly yearnings.

Her mind grew muzzy, her concentration drifted. It was *trust,* she mused. Trust. That was what set her feelings about Adam apart from those she'd had for any other man. Unlike the father who had deserted her when she was a girl, or the friends who had refused to believe she was being harassed,

Adam would always be there if she needed him. He was constant. Faithful.

It had been a long time since she'd felt this secure.

The sun had turned the western sky deep-pink and had sunk below the horizon by the time Adam decided to rouse Sara. He had a crick in his neck from leaning awkwardly against the base of the tree where they sat, and his arm had gone to sleep from lack of movement.

"Hey, sleepyhead. Time to go."

She purred, snuggled closer. Her palm slid over his chest in a drowsy caress. "Ummm…"

It had been hard enough to hold Sara in his arms without kissing her while she slept. Now, it was even harder. Half-awake, snuggled up and touching him like that, she was endearing. And irresistible. Adam was no fool. If he didn't get away from her immediately, they were both going to regret it.

Only his overblown sense of chivalry kept him from unceremoniously dumping her on the ground as he abruptly arose. "That's it. I'm out of here." Towering over her, he added, "Well? Are you coming?"

"Umm, what?" Confused, she peered up at him and yawned. "Where are we?"

"A couple of miles from home. And it's getting dark. So I suggest you get a move on."

"Okay. Sure. I was just resting my eyes."

"Yeah. Right."

She got stiffly to her feet. "What are you so grumpy about?"

"I'm not grumpy."

Sara pointed to the oak where they'd sat. "Right. And that's not a tree."

"Looks like one to me."

"My point, exactly. I know a grump when I see one, too. I just don't know what I did to set you off."

Adam had known from the start that he'd have to protect Sara from both external forces and from himself. He was up to the task. It was simply a matter of remaining focused on the important aspects of her case and overlooking the personal side. And to do that, he'd have to convince her that her continued presence had no affect on him.

"Don't give yourself so much credit," he hedged. "My mood has nothing to do with you."

Chagrined and embarrassed, she busied herself brushing dried leaves off her jeans so she wouldn't have to look at him. "Sorry. My mistake."

As Adam turned away, she let her thoughts dwell on his unfeeling statement. The worst part was, he was probably right. Ever since childhood she'd tended to blame herself if everyone around her wasn't cheerful, as if it were her job to ensure their happiness. That kind of attitude was fine for handling a class of active five-year-olds but it wasn't a very practical way to run the other parts of her life.

Eric Rydell had looked lonely and lost when she'd first met him. Was it her penchant for wanting to see people happy that had drawn her to him? Perhaps. And perhaps not. There was no way to know what had motivated Eric, any more than there was a way to read what was going on in Adam's head.

"Lou was right," Sara muttered. "I do have a lot to learn."

"About what?"

If she'd been about to be drawn and quartered by a team of wild horses, she wouldn't have told him. Instead, she made a silly, cynical face. "Are you still here?"

"Obviously."

Aggravation—at herself and at men, in general— gave her renewed vigor. "Well, what are we waiting for? It's getting dark. Let's head for home."

If Adam was surprised by her sudden spurt of energy, he gave no indication of it. That pleased Sara. It also seemed fair. Since she didn't understand *him*, there was no reason he should understand her, either.

Every time she'd started to think he might be mellowing, he'd proved her wrong, as if it gave him some kind of perverse pleasure to do so. Could she have been wrong about seeing the Lord's hand in their meeting, too? She supposed so. It wouldn't be the first time she'd presumed to know the will of God and been totally mistaken.

Leading the way, Adam chose the easiest path rather than the quickest. It was his fault Sara was so tired. He should have known better than to push her so hard. She always seemed so spunky, so capable, he tended to forget she was a novice when it came to country living.

They hadn't actually walked far, over all. It was the rough terrain that had slowed them down and made the journey seem so arduous. Tomorrow, after they'd had a good night's sleep, he'd leave her at the cabin and hike down to the store, alone. He was looking forward to being away from her, even for a short time.

On cue, Sara spoke up. "Are we lost?"

"No. Why?"

"Because I could swear we're going in the wrong direction."

"How would *you* know?"

"Ha ha. I'm being serious, Adam. Am I *that* turned around?"

"Not this time. I'm taking us around the perimeter of a hogback so we don't have to climb so much."

"I take it you mean a hill."

Adam chuckled. "Well, I'm not talking about bacon. Actually, it's kind of a ridge of hills."

Sighing deeply, Sara blinked to try to clear her vision. "It's getting harder to see."

"There's a nearly full moon tonight. It won't ever get completely dark."

"Oh, whoopee. I'm thrilled."

"Now, who's a grump?"

"Sorry." She considered for a moment, then went on. "The problem is, I hate the dark."

Adam slowed so she could catch up and walk beside him instead of trailing, as she had been. "Since when?"

"Since I was little."

"Do you have any idea why?"

It occurred to her that he'd accept any explanation, even one about children being prone to such fears. However, her heart told her to be honest, so she was. "Some of my earliest memories involve lying in bed at night and listening to my parents' angry voices. I used to imagine all kinds of awful things happening under the cover of darkness. Things like they show in horror movies. It devastated me."

"I can see where it would."

"I used to pray I'd get a brother or sister to keep me company, to share the dread. I never did."

"Having siblings just gives you something else to worry about," Adam said. "Believe me, it's highly overrated."

"Come to think of it, I've never asked.... Were

you an only child?'' Sara thought at first that he wasn't going to answer.

Finally, he said, "No. I had a younger brother."

Noting that he'd used the past tense, Sara got a feeling of foreboding. Though she hoped he'd explain further, she wasn't going to press him for details if he chose not to disclose any. There was evidently a lot of past hurt in Adam Callahan's life. A lot of disappointment. She couldn't expect him to bare all his secrets at once. It didn't really matter. A person didn't have to know everything about someone else's tragedy to offer comfort.

Soul-deep compassion flowed over and into her. Filled her. Made her reach for his hand.

Adam didn't resist. There was solace in Sara's touch. That was a gift he couldn't refuse.

He didn't try to speak. He was afraid that if he did, his voice would betray the intensity of his response to her simple act of kindness. It was as if God had sanctified the joining of their hands. Made it so sweet it was painful. Wondering if Sara had also sensed the special blessing they shared, Adam glanced over at her. She was aglow with a look of utter peace. The moon had risen behind her, making a silver halo for her beautiful, golden hair. Her skin shone like ivory. Her eyes sparkled with the brilliance of pale emeralds. It was as if she were in tune with everything around her. The entire universe.

In awe, Adam stared, then summarily rejected his

initial conclusions as ridiculous fancies. He was just overtired. So was she. That was why they seemed to need each other's moral support so much.

Sara's heart was breaking for Adam. She didn't know why. She only knew that his spiritual needs were deep and that she was supposed to comfort him. That was enough.

The physical pain and fatigue became secondary, faded away. Temporarily renewed, she kept pace and held tight to his hand. Any doubt that she belonged right where she was faded. This man needed her moral support, her blessing, her heartfelt prayers, whether he was ready to admit it or not.

It was easy to visualize a personal side to their relationship, too. That, she decided, was *not* a good idea. Not yet. First things first. Adam needed spiritual healing. Anything beyond that was up to the Lord, since He was obviously the one arranging the whole scenario.

"Is it far, now?" she finally asked.

"No. Not far. Samson's probably home already waiting for us."

"In that case, I hope he's built a fire in the stove and put on a fresh pot of coffee."

"Sorry. I don't let him play with matches."

"That's probably just as well," Sara said, smiling. "With all his hair, it could be dangerous for him to handle fire."

"Right."

Their everyday conversation had drawn her mind away from more spiritual thoughts. Reminded of her fatigue, she lagged behind.

Adam kept hold of her hand. It was hard to tell for sure in the dim light, but he thought she looked pale. And there were definite frown lines in her forehead as she struggled to keep up. "How are you doing?"

"I'm fine."

"You don't look fine."

"Thanks a heap."

"You know what I meant." He wanted to sweep her up in his arms and carry her the rest of the way to the cabin. What stopped him was remembering how much he'd loved feeling her close to him. And knowing how tempting it would be to continue to hold her once he stepped over the invisible boundary that was keeping them apart.

It was the glimmer of unshed tears in Sara's eyes that pushed him to act in spite of his misgivings. This time, though, he wasn't going to be fool enough to hold her like a lover would. He'd carry her, yes, but she was going home like a sack of potatoes.

Without a word, Adam bent over in front of her, grasped her lower legs, and threw her upper body over his shoulder.

Sara shrieked. "What are you doing?"

"Carrying you."

"No kidding."

"Stop wriggling," he warned. "I don't want to drop you."

"Why? Can't find a mud puddle?"

"Very funny."

She grimaced. "I thought so."

Adam started off. Every step he took jarred her, drove the air out of her lungs. By timing her breathing to coincide with his strides, she was able to squeak out, "This is *not* what I had in mind when I teased you about carrying me home."

"Oh? My mistake."

"So, put me down."

"In a few minutes."

"My head will have exploded in a few minutes," she argued. "Do you have any idea what it feels like to hang upside down like this?"

Adam chuckled. "No, but I'll bet you plan to tell me."

"Would it do any good?"

"Probably not."

"That's what I figured." Seeking to keep her balance in what she considered a precarious position, she stuck one thumb through the belt loops on Adam's jeans and used her other arm to grasp him around the waist. Thus stabilized, her ride became more tolerable.

Adam hadn't counted on Sara's finding yet another way to hold him. He'd toted accident victims and lawbreakers out of harm's way by carrying them like this and he'd never enjoyed it. Before now.

Well, it was your stupid idea to pick her up, so live with it, he told himself cynically. You're almost home.

And then what? Adam wondered. It had gotten so that even mundane acts drew him to Sara. That was not good.

He snorted derisively. Not good? That had to be the understatement of the century.

The last few hundred yards to the cabin were the longest Adam had ever walked. Reaching the porch, he set Sara's feet on it and steadied her until she got her balance. "Well, here we are. That wasn't so bad, was it?"

"Not considering the alternative." She stretched. "I don't know about you, but all I want to do is take off my boots and crash."

"Sounds like a sensible plan. If you're hungry, we can finish off the corn dodgers."

She made a face. "No, thanks. They tasted much better first thing this morning than they did later. I think I've had enough to last me another twenty years or so."

"They do stick to your ribs, though, don't they?" he said, chuckling. "I figured, as many as you were putting away, you'd get sick of them pretty soon."

"You're a smart man."

"I know. I keep telling you that." He opened the door and ushered her in. "Sit down and I'll pull off your boots."

"My hero."

Adam gave her a mock sneer and cocked one eyebrow. "It's about time you realized that."

"I've known it from the start," she said, sobering. "I don't know how to thank you for all you've done for me."

He wasn't about to let her draw him into a serious conversation. Not after the unsettling feelings he'd noted while carrying her home. "Shut up and stick out your foot."

"Yes, sir, Mr. Callahan." Sara sank onto the edge of the bed, leaned back, braced herself, and offered one foot.

The boot resisted. Adam gave a series of tugs to ease it off, then reached for the other one.

She sighed. "Umm. It's sure good to be home."

"Yeah. It is." He set the boots aside and pulled off her socks, as well. Seated on the floor beside the bed, he began to gently rub her feet.

"Oh, thank you," she purred. "I don't think I've ever had a massage that felt that good."

"You'll get my bill in the mail," Adam quipped. He didn't dare say what he was really thinking. Really feeling. He'd never thought of a woman's feet as attractive before. Sara's, however, were so appealing he never wanted to stop caressing them.

What was the matter with him? Was he nuts? Probably. It wouldn't be the first time he'd been accused of getting his priorities out of order.

He looked up at her face. Her eyes were closed, her lips slightly parted. In all probability, she'd just been through the most trying few days of her life, yet she was able to enjoy simple pleasures and celebrate life without dwelling on the menace that might still lay in wait for her. He'd never met anyone he admired more.

Adam got to his feet, lifted Sara's legs, and swung them around until she was lying flat on the bed. "You rest. I'll fix us a little something to eat and then we can turn in." He drew the quilted coverlet over her, tucking it up around her chin.

She tried to rise. "I'll help you."

"No," he said, gently restraining her. "Stay there. Nap if you want. I'll wake you when supper's ready."

"It's like I said, before," she whispered. "You're too good to be true."

"Yeah." He straightened, thrust his hands into his pockets to keep from touching her again. "You've got that right."

Chapter Twelve

A knock on Adam's door early the next morning startled everyone. Samson began to bark so loudly the windows rattled.

Wide-eyed, Sara pulled the quilt up under her chin and stared at the door.

"Stay where you are," Adam ordered. Already dressed, he reached for the service revolver he kept in a kitchen drawer and shoved it into his belt at the small of his back.

Laying a hand on Samson's head, he quieted him with a calm, "It's okay, boy," then stood beside the door to call out, "Who is it?"

The voice was thin, reedy. "It's me. Bobby Joe."

Sara let out her breath in a noisy whoosh. "Oh, my."

Scowling, Adam eased open the door. "How did you get here?"

"Papaw was goin' to the store so I rode along."

Adam glanced past the boy and scanned the clearing. "Okay. Then how did you get so close to the house without setting off my alarm?"

"You mean the wire?" Bobby grinned in self-satisfaction. "I thought that was for bears, or somethin'. I just stepped over it."

"Was it that obvious?"

"Was to me." He leaned aside to peer past the man. "Miss Sara here?"

"She's here." Adam opened the door farther. "Would you like to come in?"

The child was through the door like a shot. Thumping Samson on the head in passing he made straight for Sara's bed. "Morning. You sure sleep late."

"I had a rough day yesterday." She took a quick inventory of her condition beneath the quilt and discovered she was still dressed from the previous day. A handy state, considering her early-morning visitor. Apparently she'd fallen asleep the minute her head had hit the pillow and failed to change into the oversize T-shirt she'd borrowed from Adam to use as a nightgown.

Fighting typical morning moodiness, she looked over at him. "I thought you said you were going to wake me for supper."

"I tried. You weren't having any."

"I might have, if I'd been awake."

"If you'd been awake, you probably wouldn't have bitten my head off when I tried to rouse you."

"Oh, dear. Did I?"

"What do you think?"

Nodding in understanding, she threw back the quilt and swung her legs over the edge of the bed as she sat up. "I think…you're probably lucky you're feeling as good as you are this morning. I tend to be a bit cranky at times like that."

"A bit cranky? Hah!"

"Okay. A lot cranky." Casting him a dour look she said, "If you gentlemen will excuse me, I'll go freshen up. Feel free to make coffee. Lots of it."

"Yes, ma'am." Adam reached for the coffeepot as Sara hurried out of the room. He said to Bobby, "She'll be nicer when she's more awake."

"My mama's like that. 'Course, I don't see her that much."

"Is she home, now?"

"Naw. She's never around. Not since my daddy died."

Adam could certainly identify with those feelings of loss and futility; both Bobby's and his mother's. "Was that when she got the job traveling?"

"Yeah." He was wandering around the room, looking it over. "You lived here long?"

"A couple of years. How come you don't know

that? I thought everybody knew everything about everybody else up here.''

''S'pose they do.'' His grin was bright and inquisitive. ''Where do you work?''

''I don't. Not anymore.''

Bobby studied him. ''How come?''

''I'm retired.''

''Wow!'' His eyes widened. ''You don't *look* that old.''

Adam laughed. ''I'm not old. I just don't work at a regular job anymore.''

''Must be fun to go huntin' and fishin' any old time you want.'' The boy began to scratch behind Samson's ears while he talked. ''Kinda lonesome up here, though, huh?''

Adam heard the shower start, thought of Sara, and felt his body tighten, tense. In self-defense he said, ''Actually, I enjoy being by myself.''

Bobby didn't contradict him, but Adam saw doubt in the child's gaze.

The same doubt was reflected in his own heart.

By the time Sara had showered and changed into fresh clothing, she felt much better. Fixing a smile on her face she rejoined the others.

Adam immediately handed her a mug of steaming coffee. She cupped her hands around it and sipped carefully. ''Umm. I may live.''

''Let's hope so,'' he said. ''You hungry?''

"Famished." Sara winked at Bobby. "How about you?"

"Yes, ma'am."

"Good." Seating herself at the table she pretended she was ordering at a café. "My young friend and I will have pancakes, bacon and scrambled eggs. You can skip the homemade hash browns this morning."

Bobby looked at her in astonishment. "He can cook?"

"Sure can. Does a good job of it, too."

"Wow. My papaw can't even nuke cold pizza without blowing it all over the inside of the microwave. Mamaw won't let him in the kitchen. Me, either."

"Well, I will," Adam said quickly. "If you two want pancakes, I'm going to need some help. Get over here."

Sara started to rise, caught the warning look in Adam's eyes, and sank back into her chair with an understanding smile. "I'm afraid I'm not awake enough, yet. Guess you men will have to do the work. I'll volunteer to clean up afterward."

"All right." Bobby Joe was already stationed next to Adam, waiting for instructions.

"It's easy," Adam said. "You just look at the directions on the back of the mix and do what it says." He placed a bowl and measuring cup on the counter. "Make enough for four. Miss Sara's a big eater."

The boy's shoulders sagged. "I could fry the bacon, instead."

"Too dangerous. It might splatter and burn you." Adam got his part of the meal started, then crouched down to Bobby Joe's level and pointed to the box. "See? The pictures do most of the work. Grab the measuring cup and I'll pour."

Reluctantly, the boy complied. "I don't know...."

"Sure, you do. Take it one step at a time. It's just like fishing. You have to do things in the right order. You wouldn't put a worm on the hook *after* you'd caught your fish, would you?"

"Not unless I wanted to catch another fish," Bobby said wisely.

"Okay. Maybe that was a bad example." Adam glanced over his shoulder at Sara and found her stifling a case of the giggles. "Think of it as getting dressed, then. You start with your socks, then put your shoes on."

"'Cept in the summer. I don't wear shoes, then."

Adam looked back at Sara. "Maybe *you* should do this."

She waved his comment away with her free hand. The other was clamped firmly over her mouth while her shoulders shook with suppressed laughter. "You're doing fine."

Frustrated, Adam turned back to the boy and pointed to the instructions. "Okay. See the number one?"

"Uh-huh." Bobby leaned closer and squinted.

"That's for the mix. We'll need three cups of that. You pour."

The boy managed to get a fair amount of the powdery pancake mix from the box to the cup to the bowl. Proud of himself, he beamed up at Adam through a cloud of flour. "Now what?"

"Check number two. My bacon's burning."

By the time he'd rescued the frying pan, Bobby was trying to pour milk into the cup. Being so short, he was having trouble lifting the heavy milk carton and tipping it at the same time.

Sara was sorely tempted to help but she knew the child would feel much better about himself if he managed alone. Adam apparently agreed because he merely stood back and watched.

"It said two cups," Bobby told his mentor solemnly. He pointed. "See?"

"You're right," Adam said. "Want me to break the eggs for you?"

"I can do it."

"Okay. Go for it."

Sara held her breath. She was going to eat those pancakes, even if they had bits of shell in them, but she'd rather they didn't, just the same. When she heard Bobby say, "Oops," and, "Uh-oh," she was pretty sure there was going to be a surprise crunchiness in the batch. Oh, well, it was worth it if he gained confidence.

Sipping her coffee, she watched man and boy work together. Adam was good with children once he set aside his practiced gruffness and let himself act naturally. He'd make some lucky kid a *great* father.

That idea caught her by surprise. It flowed through her, warming her from the inside out, like the hot coffee trickling down her throat. *Father. Mother. Child. A happy family.* Was it too outlandish a hope to see herself in that kind of a permanent situation?

She immediately discounted the concept. With her rotten track record, there was no way she could trust her instincts. Even if she was able to convince herself she and Adam might be compatible, that didn't make it so. No amount of wishing could change the facts. Not that she had the slightest idea what the facts really were.

Sara realized she was being overly cynical. Did that mean she wasn't putting her full confidence in her Heavenly Father? Probably. Deriding herself she muttered, "So, what else is new?"

Adam glanced over his shoulder. "I beg your pardon?"

"Um, the pancakes," she said. "Are they ready?"

He smiled knowingly. "Pretty soon. Why don't you set the table for us? And use lots of dishes."

"Why?" She was still so distracted by her disturbing thoughts she didn't see what he was getting at.

"Because this time I don't have to wash them," Adam said with a chuckle. He elbowed Bobby Joe. "After breakfast, some of us are going fishing."

Sara raised her eyebrows. "And I get to stay home and play Cinderella? No fair."

"You can do it barefoot," Adam reminded her. "That should sound good if your feet are still sore."

Bobby tugged on his shirtsleeve. "Mamaw read me that story. If you were a prince and Miss Sara was wearing glass slippers, you could marry her, huh?"

Flustered, Adam turned back to his tasks at the stove without comment while Sara giggled in the background. It wasn't funny to him. People he'd cared about had been ripped from his life. No way was he going to weaken and let it happen again.

He'd thought this whole problem through many times. As far as he was concerned, the only way to keep his heart in one piece was to isolate himself. To turn away from everyone. To live as he had been, alone and unhindered by unnecessary attachments.

Was that what Sara was? he wondered. Was that all she was to him? An unnecessary attachment?

Rather than answer his own question he closed

his mind to it. It didn't matter what he thought. What he felt. She'd made it clear she was only using him as a makeshift bodyguard. Fine. He could accept that. To consider anything else was a fool's notion, anyway.

Rain postponed the planned fishing trip. Sara found it interesting that Adam seemed so upset about the storm. She'd listened to him talking to Bobby Joe while she washed the dishes but nothing in his conversation helped her understand what was bothering him so much.

When she was finished, she got out her laptop computer and sat down on the sofa. "Okay, Bobby. Cinderella's finished in the kitchen. Unless there are floors to mop or windows to wash, I can play now."

"Okay." He joined her. "You gonna plug that thing in?"

"No. It runs on batteries." She turned it on. "See? No wires."

"Wow. Got any good games on it?"

"If you mean the kind that go *boom,* no. But we can play some word games."

He edged away. "Naw. That's okay."

Sara remembered the way he'd peered at the instructions on the pancake mix box. That gave her an idea. "Wait. Look. I can make the letters really big." Judging by the way the boy's eyes lit up when she manipulated the images on the screen, she decided she was on to something. Maybe his learning problems weren't what she'd assumed, at all.

Handing him the keyboard, she said, "How's that? Can you see it when it's enlarged like that?"

"Yeah."

"Well, write something. How about your name?"

Curious, Adam approached and squeezed himself in on the other side of the boy, watching as he laboriously searched for the right keys and entered his name. Looking over Bobby's head, he caught Sara's attention and mouthed, "Glasses?"

She nodded. "I think so." After complimenting Bobby Joe on his typing skills, she asked, "Have you ever had your eyes checked, honey?"

"I dunno."

Something about his answer gave her pause. "You wouldn't fib to me, would you?"

He hung his head and acted ashamed. "No, ma'am. I...I had glasses but I broke 'em. Twice. My mother said if I did it again, I couldn't have another pair."

"So you didn't tell her, right? How about your grandmother? Does she know about this?"

"I dunno. Maybe."

"Bobby..."

He shook his head. "No, ma'am. I never told her either."

"Then it was a real blessing I got stranded here." Sara could tell the boy wasn't convinced. "You don't have to tell Lou yourself. I can talk to her for you if you want me to.''

''Do we have to?''

''Yes, we do. It would be awful to have you get any more behind in school.''

''I don't care. I hate school.''

Adam spoke up. ''So did I.''

''No kidding?'' The child's head whipped around, his eyes wide in amazement.

''No kidding. It seemed like a real waste of time until I decided I wanted to know about motorcycle racing and African safaris and sailing around the world. You know. All kinds of stuff. I found out that if I could read, I could learn how to do all kinds of things and grow up to be anything I wanted to be.''

''I guess so.'' He brightened. ''Or I could just stay retired, like you.''

Both adults laughed. Adam said, ''I'm afraid it doesn't work quite that way. You have to have a job first.''

''Yeah, I figured. What did you used to do?''

''I was a policeman.''

''Really? Wow! I'll bet that was fun, huh?''

Adam got to his feet. Turned away. Stuffed his hands in his pockets. ''It was good to be able to help people who were in trouble.'' He started for the door, then realized the rain was going to keep him inside whether he liked it or not. Talk about *trapped*.

Sara sensed his discomfiture and changed the subject. "While I'm here, Bobby, maybe you and I can use the computer to help you catch up a little on your reading skills. I promise we'll stop when you want to."

He shrugged his thin shoulders. "Okay, I guess."

"You know, it's lucky for you that I wound up stuck out here. Because I'm a teacher, I mean."

Wisely, the boy agreed. "Yeah. I guess Jesus was looking out for me, huh?"

"I guess He was." Sara smiled sweetly. "I'm glad you reminded me of that. Sometimes I forget."

"Do you go to church?"

She didn't slant the truth to try to protect her image as a practicing Christian. "I used to."

"Mamaw says you got to keep going to church and readin' the Bible. She says it's like starvin' to death if you don't stay in the Word."

"I suspect you're right. When I get home, I promise you I'll start going to church, again. Okay?"

"Don't have to wait that long," Bobby said excitedly. "We're havin' a brush arbor meeting next Sunday. There's gonna be dinner-on-the-ground after, and gospel singin' and everything."

"Oh, I'd *love* to go to that." She looked to Adam. "Could we?"

His back was to her. He didn't turn. "You can do whatever you want."

"No, I mean, would you take me?" Thinking of

the possibility that Eric was still in the neighborhood, she was reluctant to promise the eager child anything unless she was sure she could fulfill that promise. Besides, it seemed a perfect opportunity to involve Adam with the local community, at least on a social level.

"I doubt it'll be necessary for me to go with you," Adam said flatly. "Sunday is still days away. I'm sure I'll have heard from my friends by then."

"But, if you don't…"

He whirled, his jaw set, his spine stiff. "We'll worry about that when the time comes. Okay?"

"Okay." Sara hoped she looked indifferent enough when she shrugged and pretended to relax. She'd never seen Adam so uncompromising. Clearly, he didn't intend to go to the brush arbor meeting. The question was, why? And why did his voice turn so harsh when she'd pressed him about it?

Quieting her spirit, Sara prayed silently for guidance while Bobby played with the computer. *What's wrong with Adam, Father? And how can I help him?*

There was a sensitive soul hidden beneath his carefully controlled persona. She knew there was. And her heart told her he was crying out to belong again, in spite of his defiance.

But belong to what? To society? To the police force? To the family he didn't seem to have and wouldn't talk about?

To God, came the clear answer. Of course. Tears of sympathy filled Sara's eyes. Adam, himself, had told her he'd turned away from his beliefs. Whether he admitted it or not, he was alienated from the peace he sought because he chose to be. It didn't matter what had happened to disillusion him. God was big enough to handle any crisis. The key to anyone's recovery was in turning the outcome over to the Lord and trusting Him for healing.

Sara nodded slowly, finally comprehending. No wonder Adam didn't want to go to the brush arbor meeting with her. It wasn't her he was angry with. And it wasn't society he was hiding from. It was God.

Peace flowed over and through her. If her car hadn't slid off the road in the first place, if other circumstances hadn't forced her to stay on at Adam's, she'd never have understood. Never have had a chance to help him, if only by example.

Her first instinct had been to try to coerce him into going to the church meeting with her. But she thought better of it. It wouldn't do any good to drag him along against his will. If his heart wasn't ready to forgive the Lord, for whatever reason, there was nothing she could do about it. Adam's problems were between him and God.

Sara's urge to interfere was strong. It was hard to keep silent. Hard to step out of the way and let the

Lord have His way with Adam. She closed her eyes and asked for strength. For wisdom.

"But not patience," she muttered, her lips barely moving. "The last time I asked for that, I nearly went crazy."

Analyzing her current situation she began to smile. Maybe the divine lesson in forbearance wasn't over yet.

Chapter Thirteen

Sara was afraid she and Adam would have to walk Bobby Joe all the way home. Instead, the boy finally admitted he was supposed to meet his grandfather at Burnham's store around three that afternoon.

"I can take him over, alone," Adam said.

Bobby piped up, "I don't need any help walkin' back. I never get lost."

"Unlike your friend, Miss Sara," Adam said with a self-satisfied smile. "She can get lost going out to my shed for wood."

"Hey, I'm not *that* bad." Sara made a silly face at her two companions, concentrating most of the mockery on Adam. "I got there and back okay, once."

"And then hit me in the head with a log when I tried to help you." He rubbed the spot. "I know it doesn't show anymore, but it hurts when I press on it hard.''

"Then don't press on it," she countered, her voice overly sugary.

Bobby joined in. "That's what Mamaw always says."

"Undoubtedly." Adam was smiling down at him. "It sounds to me like your grandmother has a saying for just about everything."

"Just about. She's real smart." He searched the man's face. "Didn't you have a mamaw?"

"A long time ago I did. I don't remember her, though."

"That's too bad. How 'bout your mom and pop? Do they live around here?"

Adam shook his head. "No. They used to have a place near Chicago. That's where I'm from. A few years ago they sold it and moved to Florida."

"Oh."

Seeing the boy nodding wisely and making a sour face, Adam asked, "What's wrong?"

"Nothing."

"Come on. You and I are buddies. What's the matter?" He crouched down to put himself on Bobby's level.

"It's okay," the boy said. "I like you even if you are a Yankee. You can't help it if it makes you contrary. Mamaw says..."

"I don't doubt she does." Laughing, Adam

straightened. He sent a pointed look at Sara. "You might be surprised how many really nice Yankees there are in these parts. Some of them are kind of pretty, too. When they're not all covered with mud."

Sara didn't wait for Bobby to figure out what Adam was hinting at. "I'm from up there, too," she said. "And I'm not nearly as cranky as Mr. Callahan."

"'Cept in the morning," Bobby reminded her.

She laughed. "You're right. Except in the morning. So, what have we decided? Do I need to grab my boots and keep you two company or can you do without me?"

Bobby looked forlorn. "You don't want to come?"

"I do, but..." Slipping her sock off one heel she displayed the blisters she gotten on the previous day's trek. "I could use a little more time to heal."

"Ooh." He sounded impressed. "That looks sore."

"Not if I don't press on it too hard," Sara teased, emulating Adam's faulty reasoning and getting the child to smile. "It's just less painful if I don't have to wear those boots right now."

"No kidding."

Adam pulled on a light, waterproof jacket. "I think you've convinced our guest. Just stay put. I'll be back soon."

"While you're at Burnham's..."

"I know," he said. "I'll check for messages and see what I can do about getting a heavy-duty tow for my truck. Anything else we need?"

"Not that I know of." She gazed out the window over the sink. "Looks like the rain's stopped."

"For now. Probably slicked up that patch of bad road where you parked, though."

Sara smiled wryly. "Where *we* parked, you mean?"

"Yeah. Where *we* parked." Adam scowled. "I haven't done anything that dumb in a long time."

"It probably happened because you got mad. I usually make my worst mistakes when I let my emotions take charge of my brain."

Sobering, Adam nodded. His eyes held an unspoken sorrow. "You're right. That's why I left the force. Logic had started taking second place to my gut feelings."

"And that can be dangerous, can't it?"

After a long pause, Adam said, "Yes. It can be deadly."

Sara was relieved to spend some time away from Adam while he and Samson walked Bobby to the store. Her conversations with the enigmatic man always seemed to get overly profound in the blink of an eye and she was tired of worrying what she might say next that would set him off. Make him miserable. The feeling wasn't exactly like walking on egg-shells. It was more a matter of navigating the Arctic Ocean filled with icebergs.

"In a leaky boat," she added out loud. Adam was exasperating. The man had a quick wit and an enjoyable, wry sense of humor—when he wasn't brooding. When his mood plummeted, however, she found herself yearning to take him in her arms, to rock him like a sorrowing child until the hurt went away.

Sara shivered. Would there never be an end to her gullibility? Ever since she was little she'd taken needy things under her wing. Homeless animals. Friendless children. And finally Eric Rydell. Eric's loneliness had drawn her, as if her compassion were all that mattered. Only he hadn't understood that, had he?

"I never meant to hurt you, Eric," she whispered. "I just wanted you to share in the happiness I'd found." Which was why she'd taken him to church with her in the first place. Everything would have been fine if only he hadn't confused her Christian love and concern with the other kind. The carnal kind.

Sara remembered the last semi-normal conversation they'd had. She and Eric had been chaperoning a group of teenagers in the church youth group. He'd brought her home late afterward, and tarried on the front porch.

"I really have to go in," Sara had said.

Eric had grabbed her, instead, and kissed her. When she hadn't responded the way he'd thought she should, he'd become angry. "You've been flirting with me all night. Don't you dare turn me down now."

"I thought we were friends," Sara countered.

"Sure. That, too." He still had his hands on her shoulders. His grasp tightened. His dark eyes narrowed. The thin mustache turned up slightly at the ends as he leered at her. "Only I'm tired of being patient, Sara. You owe me a lot more than friendship."

She tried to twist free. "I don't owe you a thing."

Once again, he pulled her to him. Held her so tight she was breathless. Frightened. He tried to force another kiss on her. She closed her teeth on his lower lip, instead.

Eric jumped away, cursing. His hand tested his injured mouth. "You bit me!" He drew back to hit her, then apparently thought better of it. "Don't you dare do anything like that again. You hear?"

Trembling, Sara began backing toward the sanctuary of her front door. "I won't."

"That's better." Eric smirked. "I knew you were a smart girl."

"If I was smart, I'd never have gotten involved with you in the first place."

"But you did," he countered. "You started this and you're going to finish it."

Reaching behind her back, Sara had grasped the knob of the door and turned it slowly, silently. Almost free, she'd thought. Almost safe.

Recalling that horrible evening she could taste fresh fear. Her heart responded by racing. Her breathing was labored. Just like back then.

"I'm not going to finish anything, Eric," she'd managed to reply as she'd jerked open the door, ducked through, and slammed it in his face. Safe inside, she'd slid the dead bolt home as she'd called out, "I never want to see you again."

Eric's fists had hit the door with such force it had vibrated violently. "Nobody gives me the brush-off," he'd shouted. "Nobody. You'll be sorry, you hear? You'll be sorry."

Sara remembered trembling, bracing her shoulder against the door, praying he wouldn't get through. Although he'd eventually stopped pounding and left, that was the night her joy had been stolen. That was the moment his campaign of intimidation had begun.

And now, here she was. In the middle of nowhere. Alone. Wide-eyed, she sized up the doors of Adam's cabin. They had no locks. No bolts. Nothing. If Eric found her there, she'd be helpless.

Oh, how she wished she'd asked Adam to leave Samson with her for protection instead of insisting the enormous dog needed more exercise.

"It's my *brain* that needs exercise," Sara grumbled. She cast around for a way to bar the doors, settling on pushing a storage cabinet in front of the one in the back. She upended the dining table across the front door and piled chairs behind it for weight.

All in all, her efforts were pretty feeble. She knew that. But she couldn't sit there and wait for her nemesis to show up without doing something to deter his attack. If he came through the doors, anyway, she'd just have to conk him with a hunk of firewood to slow him down.

At least she knew that worked.

Adam delivered Bobby to the store and insisted on phoning his grandfather to make sure he was really coming. Lou assured him that her husband, Seth, would fetch the boy around three, as promised.

That was good enough for Adam. Leaving Bobby with a bag of penny candy to keep him occupied, he started for home.

Samson made several brief forays into the woods to tree squirrels. Each time Adam called him back. "I don't have time to chase after you," he told the dog. "Sara's waiting."

Samson wagged his bushy tail and panted, his lips drawn back in a doggy grin.

"Yes, I said, *Sara*," Adam drawled. "I think you're going to miss her as much as I am."

When Samson replied with an amiable, "Broof," Adam read plenty into it.

"You don't have to rub it in. I know what I just said. Yes, you old cynic, I will miss her. But don't you dare breathe a word of it to Sara, you hear? It's going to be bad enough as it is."

"Broof, broof!"

"Oh, shut up," Adam said in disgust. "I know it's all my fault. I should have sent her on her way the first time I saw her." He scowled down at the Great Pyrenees as he added, "Come to think of it, you're the one who started this. It's *your* fault."

Samson looked terribly pleased with himself. Adam could have sworn the dog was gloating.

Afternoon shadows lengthened. Sara huddled in a corner of the room, her back to the wall, her eyes focused on the front door. She'd tried to read. Tried to use the laptop computer. Nothing was distracting enough to hold her attention for more than a few minutes.

Suddenly, she heard a man's footsteps on the porch. The doorknob turned. The door banged hard against the upended table.

Caught by surprise, she screamed.

The door hit harder. Wood splintered. Furniture skittered across the floor.

"Sara!"

It was Adam's voice. *Thank God.* Sara answered, "I'm here. Wait. I'll move the table."

He was making such a ruckus trying to get past her barricade that he didn't hear anything else. With one last mighty surge he burst into the room. The moment he saw her, alive and well, he was so relieved he forgot all his prior misgivings, leaped over the scattered chairs, and immediately enfolded her in his thankful embrace.

Sara was equally relieved. All she wanted to do was stay right where she was, held safe in Adam's strong arms, for as long as she lived. Maybe longer.

Blinking back tears of joy she clung to him, her head on his shoulder, her arms around his waist. "I missed you."

"I can see that." It seemed the most natural thing in the world to place a conciliatory kiss on her hair before he loosened his hold. Then, speaking gently, he cupped her face in his hands and tilted it up so he could look into her misty gaze. "Why was all the furniture piled in front of the door?"

"I was rearranging it?"

"Don't give me that. Nobody stacks the dining room in a heap."

"It's a new fashion?"

Adam huffed. "If you didn't look so scared, I might buy that excuse from you, considering."

"Considering what?" Sara was so glad to see him she could barely restrain herself from raising on tiptoe and kissing him solidly, no matter how often he'd denied any tender feelings for her.

"Considering the fact that you never give me a straight answer."

"Who, me?"

"Yes, you. You scared the life out of me. The least you can do is tell me why."

Her shoulders slumped, her balance tenuous. "It's my own fault. I have too vivid an imagination. I got to thinking about being here all alone and I remembered some of the threats Eric had made. That made me jumpy."

"So you barricaded the door."

"Uh-huh. I'm sorry about the table. I'll refinish it if it needs it."

"It needed *that* before I hit it with the door," Adam said. He slipped his arm around Sara's shoulders and guided her to the sofa. "You'd better sit down before you faint."

"I never faint."

"My mistake. Okay, how about we sit down for my sake then? My heart's beating so hard you could probably hear it from across the room."

She snuggled in the crook of his arm as he settled them both on the sofa. "I'll take your word for it. I like it fine right where I am, thank you. I'm not going anywhere. Not even across the room."

Laying her hand on his chest, she felt the racing of his pulse. It echoed hers. Fright could do that, she supposed. So could love. It was nice to pretend Adam's heart was beating fast because he cared for her, not because he'd simply been unnerved by the barred door.

There goes my vivid imagination again, she told herself. But knowing she should release the dream and actually doing it were two different things. Closing her eyes, she cuddled closer to Adam and gave her deepest wishes free rein.

Surely, it couldn't hurt to hope just a little.

It was nearly dark by the time they parted. Adam wasn't willing to break their comforting contact. Neither was Sara. In the end, it was Samson's loud demand for admittance that brought them back to reality.

Adam glanced at the front door. It had bounced off the table and slammed closed after he'd vaulted through. "I think the dog is mad at us."

"Sounds like it." She stretched languidly. "Umm. I hate to move."

"Well, it's that or get a new door. He's about to scratch through that one. I'll let him in the back. It'll be quicker."

"Not necessarily." Sara smiled over at him and fluttered her lashes theatrically. "I fixed that door, too."

"What in the world did you find to put in front of it? The washing machine?"

Her eyes widened. "Ooh. Good idea. Wish I'd thought of it. Of course, it's on the outside, so it wouldn't really help that much."

"Not unless you wanted to wash Eric to death," Adam teased.

"I can see the headlines now, 'Assailant Comes Clean.' How perfect." She sobered. "I wish it was that easy."

"It may be," Adam said. He got to his feet and began righting ladder-back chairs to move them out of the way.

Sara joined him and helped. "Did you hear from your friends? Is that it?"

"Yes. I called while I was at Burnham's. They haven't found any priors for Rydell. That, alone, is good news."

"I'll say. What do we do now?"

Adam smiled at her. "Besides fix the furniture, you mean?"

She took a mock swing at him. "Yes, silly. Besides fix the furniture."

"Oh. Well, I also tried to get a tow, again. They were just about to try the trip till this last rain postponed it again. They said to be patient another couple of days. If the road dries out enough, they'll get my truck out of the way, then work on your rental car."

Sara giggled. "I'd forgotten about your truck."

"Well, I hadn't. Turns out everybody for miles around has heard how I got stuck, too."

"Sorry about that."

"It was my own fault. I should have known better."

"Sounds like the story of my life," she said, wanting him to identify with her. "Making mistakes is my hobby. I'm just thankful the Lord's looking out for me or I'd be a goner for sure."

Watching Adam's profile, she noted a hardening of his features, a clamping of his jaw muscles. What a shame it was to hold so much useless animosity inside when both forgiveness and understanding waited for him in the person of Jesus.

She sighed, resigned to the situation. There was absolutely nothing she could do for Adam unless— until—he gave up his anger. Until he admitted what was really wrong and turned it over to the Lord.

What is really wrong? she asked herself. She didn't have a clue. Which was just as well. The less she knew about Adam Callahan's complex emotional state, the more cautious, the more aloof, she'd have to remain—for her own sake. It was scary how much she already cared for him.

Sara groaned in self-derision. *Cared* for him? That was a seriously flawed conclusion, if not an outright lie. In her opinion, she was already head over heels in love with her mysterious benefactor. Talk about making mistakes.

Chapter Fourteen

Adam had been haunted by thoughts of actually attending the brush arbor meeting with Sara ever since she'd asked him to accompany her.

He'd entertained the notion of forbidding her to go, for safety's sake, then derided himself for even considering it. Sara Stone was not the kind of person who took orders well. If at all.

He broached the subject the next morning, waiting until she'd finished two cups of coffee and started on a third. "Do you really have your heart set on going to that outdoor church meeting with Bobby Joe?"

A flutter of nervous excitement skittered through her. "I want to go, yes."

"A lot?" He paused. "I mean, is your mind made up?"

Raising one eyebrow she peered at him across the breakfast table. "That's a leading question if I ever heard one. What is it you're asking?"

"I'm just not sure you should do it, that's all. For safety's sake, I mean."

"I thought you said Eric had no police record."

"Apparently, he doesn't."

"So? What's the problem? Even if you don't want to go, there's no good reason why I shouldn't. Is there?"

"I guess not. Providing you don't get lost in the woods on your way."

Sara grinned over at him. "Hey. As long as there's no big bad wolf in the forest, I'm not worried. Has Farley seen Eric again? Has anybody?"

"No. And we're not even sure it was him the first time, except for what happened to the stuff in your car."

"Don't remind me. I wonder if we can salvage any of the gear he threw over the bank."

"It's possible. When the tow truck gets your car out of the way, I can let myself down on a rope and see."

"Well, don't try it until you're sure it's safe," Sara warned. "I wouldn't want you to get hurt." The odd look in Adam's eyes made her add, "Who'd make my breakfast if you broke a leg or something?"

"You could eat the leftover corn dodgers."

"No, thanks. I'll stick with plain pancakes. Which reminds me. Before I leave here, I want to reimburse you for all you've spent on me." She glanced around the sparsely furnished cabin. "It's not fair for me to eat your food and use up your supplies without making restitution."

"Nonsense. It was my pleasure."

"That's not what you said when Samson led you to me." It pleased Sara to see a smile begin to lift the corners of Adam's appealing mouth.

"I was having a bad night."

"*You* were having a bad night? What about me?"

"You were a pretty funny sight," he said, chuckling.

She laughed with him. "That I was. I wonder if there's any way I can salvage my skirt to wear to church?"

"I wouldn't count on it. I think it was ripped, as well as muddy."

"That's what I thought. Which is why I just left it in a heap on the porch instead of throwing it in the wash with my other things."

"Maybe Bobby's mother has a dress you could borrow."

"There isn't anything in the box of clothes Jean left here?"

Adam swallowed wrong and coughed. "Gene? A dress?"

Afraid she'd overstepped the bounds of common

courtesy, she backed down. "I'm sorry. I shouldn't have asked."

In a moment, Adam's eyes widened with comprehension. "You thought..." He coughed again. "Oh, that's rich. Gene would have loved to hear that one. He always did have a good sense of humor."

"He?" Confused, Sara frowned. "Jean's a woman's name."

"It is if you spell it with a *J*," Adam said. "My brother's name was G-e-n-e. With a *G*."

Sara looked down at the clothes she was wearing. "In that case, how come all this stuff fits?"

"My brother was a little guy. Besides, you said the waist was too big."

"It is, it is."

"Well?" Adam was still amused. "Don't look so embarrassed. It was a natural misunderstanding. You told me making mistakes was your hobby."

"No kidding." Sara waited for Adam to explain why he'd saved a box of his brother's clothes when they were of no use to him.

Instead of elaborating, however, Adam swung their conversation back to the brush arbor meeting. "I'll make a special trip to the store and check one more time before you go to the meeting. If there's nothing else to worry about, I'm sure it'll be okay for you to go alone."

"I might get lost," Sara said, still hoping he'd relent and accompany her.

"Bobby Joe said he was coming back to visit tomorrow. When he does, we'll ask him to walk you down Sunday morning. You can take Samson along for extra protection, if you want. You won't need me."

The day I don't need you will be long time coming, Sara thought. Instead of admitting it, she said, "Okay. You're the expert. If you say it's safe, then I believe you. I'll go by myself."

Noting how relieved Adam looked, she felt a surge of depression. A sense of loss. It was much easier to trust the Lord with her life when all was going according to her fondest wishes. The hard part was putting her faith to work when she was disheartened. Like now.

Adam had obviously convinced himself she'd be safe making the trek through the woods without his protection. That much was acceptable. She just hoped his conclusions had been reached from an ex-cop's viewpoint, not because he simply didn't want to go with her.

Sara brooded all day. By evening, she'd decided the best thing to do was to distance herself from Adam before she actually had to leave. Otherwise, their parting was going to hurt like crazy. It already did. The mere thought of never seeing him again was enough to cause her physical pain.

She excused herself and went to bed early, hoping

sleep would offer the relief she sought. Adam took his usual place on the floor by the wood-burning stove, even though the weather had warmed up and they hadn't built a fire in days. Samson lay beside Sara's bed, snoring.

Drifting between waking and sleeping, she heard a moan. Her eyes snapped open. She listened. Tensed. Samson continued to snore, apparently unconcerned.

The sound repeated. Deepened. Sara sat upright, clutching the covers to her chest. In the moonlight from the window she could see Adam tossing and turning on his pallet. He mumbled, groaned, then began to weep softly.

Sara slid out of bed, careful to avoid the sleeping dog, and tiptoed across the floor to where Adam lay. His hands were fisted around his blanket and there was a look of such desperate agony on his face it tore at her heart.

She dropped to her knees beside him, unsure of what to do. Clearly, he was still asleep. If she woke him when he was in such an agitated state, might he lash out at her before he realized he'd been having a nightmare?

"No," Adam mumbled. "No. Wrong. Not him, please."

Brokenhearted for the sleeping man, Sara reached to touch his brow and discovered he was perspiring.

She stroked his forehead, smoothed back his damp hair. "Adam?"

He clutched the blanket more tightly, whipped his head from side to side. "No! No!"

"Hush. It's all right. It's over. I'm here."

"Nooo!" Adam sat bolt upright, nearly knocking Sara over. His eyes flew open. He was breathing as if he'd just run a marathon.

She reeled back, then regained her balance and laid a steadying hand on his shoulder. "It's okay. It was just a dream."

"So real," he whispered. "Oh, dear God. It was just like the day it happened."

Without thought, she enfolded him in a comforting embrace, calming him with murmurs of assurance, running her hands over his back to soothe away the bad memories.

Adam held her as if he were clinging to a life raft in a hurricane. In the back of his mind he knew he shouldn't touch her at all, yet he couldn't make himself let go. Sara was warm. Real. A connection with the here and now. Proof that the past couldn't hurt him anymore.

He blinked back the tears that were still sliding down his cheeks and buried his face in her silky hair. No one else had ever seen his grief. No one had ever been trusted enough. Until now.

Adam placed a kiss in her hair and continued to hold her tight. "I'm sorry."

"For what?" Sara caressed his back through the thin cotton of his T-shirt.

"For scaring you." He sighed, shuddered. "I haven't had that dream for years. When we talked about Gene, it must have triggered the memory."

Easing away slightly, sitting back on her heels, Sara reached up to cradle his damp cheek. "What happened to him?"

"I don't..."

"Adam," she said, her voice gentle, "talk to me."

He pulled her close once again so she couldn't see his face, and spoke into the stillness. "He always said he wanted to be like me. Join the force and be a cop someday. He was just a kid. Full of hope and full of fun."

Pausing, he wondered if he should go on. If his confidant had been anyone but Sara Stone, he wouldn't have. "One day, Gene decided to dress up in my uniform and tease me about it. He knew it was against policy but he didn't care about stuff like that. Not at eighteen.

"What he didn't know was that somebody was gunning for me. When Gene walked out in the backyard in my uniform, somebody mistook him for me and shot him."

"Oh, Adam." Sara held him, rocking slightly. "I'm so sorry." *Please, Father,* she prayed, unsure of what else to say or do, *help me. Help Adam.*

"He lingered for two days," Adam continued. "I lived at the hospital. Never left him."

Sara felt him tense as he continued.

"I prayed like I'd never prayed before. Got on my knees and begged God to save him. He died in my arms."

There was nothing she could say or do to change what had happened. It was not the time for supposedly comforting platitudes. Some anguish was so deep, so profound, only time and God's grace could heal it.

Sara kissed his damp cheek, saying nothing. Her intense compassion spoke for her, spurred her to share the only solace she could offer.

Adam kissed her back tenderly, accepting the empathy she offered. This was the first time he'd been able to talk about Gene so openly and it felt as if a tremendous weight had been lifted from his broken heart.

Sara was awed by the beauty of the moment. If she hadn't had the accident that had brought her here in the first place, she'd have never met Adam, never have found out what she was missing.

Sara desperately wanted to tell him how much she loved him. He was all that mattered. He was her world. Her entire universe. When he softly whispered her name, she almost gave in and her confessed her deepest feelings.

Suddenly, a cold, wet object touched the small of her back. Sara jumped away with a shrill, ''Eeek!''

Her momentum knocked Adam back onto his pillow. Looking up, all he could see was a blur as Sara scrambled to her feet and pulled down the long shirt. Samson stood beside them, panting and looking innocent.

Adam reached for her. He was breathing hard. ''Come on back. It's just the stupid dog.''

Trembling all over, Sara stared down at him. What had she almost done?! If Samson hadn't startled her, she might have thrown away the precious gift she'd vowed to save for marriage. *Might* have, nothing. She *would* have.

''Oh, my! Oh, dear, I...'' She fought to regain her poise.

''It's my fault,'' Adam said. ''I should have remembered how he gets when he hears your name.'' He patted the place next to him. ''You must be freezing. Come here.''

Sara wrapped her arms around herself and shook her head. ''Uh-uh. I know a rescue when I see one.''

''A what?'' He was frowning.

''A rescue.'' She laid her hand on the top of Samson's broad head and ruffled his ears. ''You may think this is just a dog but I suspect he's my guardian angel in disguise.''

Raising himself on one elbow, Adam said, ''What are you talking about?''

"I never meant to get carried away like that. It's not right," she said, blushing and shivering with the vivid recollection.

"It felt pretty right to me."

"Just because it *feels* right doesn't make it so," she argued. "All I wanted to do was comfort you after your horrible nightmare and..."

"You kissed me because you felt *sorry* for me?" Adam was indignant. "I don't believe it."

She didn't know how she could explain her motives when she didn't fully understand them, herself. "I kissed you because I *care* about you," she said. "Is that so hard to accept?"

"Would you have done it if I hadn't told you about losing my brother?"

"I don't know." Sara paced across the room, then whirled. "I don't even know what I'm doing here in the first place. And don't tell me it's because of the accident with my car. You and I both know there's a lot more to it than that."

"You may think so," Adam said flatly. "I disagree."

"Fine. Be stubborn. Stay blind to divine providence if that's what makes you happy. Just don't expect me to agree with you."

"*I'm* stubborn?" he shouted. "Lady, you're the most unreasonable person I've ever met."

"Well, hopefully, you won't have to put up with me for much longer."

"Thank goodness."

Sara gritted her teeth. "In your case, Mr. Callahan, I doubt that *goodness* has anything to do with it."

In the morning, Sara awoke filled with guilt. Adam had taken her in when she'd been stranded and asked for nothing in return.

Hiding, she snuggled down in the bed and pulled the covers over her head. What could she say to him, how could she face him, after her angry outburst during the night?

She listened, expecting to hear him puttering around in the kitchen. The cabin was quiet. Not even Samson's snoring broke the silence. Chancing a peek, she lowered a little of the blanket and looked out with one eye. She was alone.

"Adam?" She sat up in bed. "Samson?"

There was no answer. It didn't smell like there was any coffee brewed, either. Climbing out of bed she wrapped the coverlet around her shoulders and trailed it across the room to the stove. The old blue-and-white, enamelware coffeepot was empty. Adam sure knew how to get even with her, didn't he?

Sara stared at the dry pot and grumbled to herself. It was obvious she should have paid more attention when he was making their coffee because she had no idea how many measures of grounds to use or how long to boil them.

A noise on the porch startled her. She whirled, pot in hand. Samson bounded through the door, followed by Adam. Sara held tight to the coverlet.

Adam gave her a cynical smile. "You planning to wear *that* to church tomorrow?"

She acknowledged how ridiculous she must look. "No, I was just pretending I was a fairy princess and I needed a flowing cape."

"I see. Well, you'll be happy to hear that they'll be up to get your car sometime late today."

"How do you know?"

"I've been down to the store," he said. "They'll tow both our vehicles to Burnham's Store. We can pick them up there."

"Wonderful." Sara's voice belied her true feelings.

"You don't sound as thrilled as I thought you'd be."

"It's not that," she said. "It's just that I'd promised Bobby I'd go to the brush arbor meeting with him. Would it be all right if I spent one more night with you, then left right after church?"

Adam took a deep breath and released it noisily. "I guess so. We've made it this far. One more night probably won't kill me."

"Especially if I leave you alone," Sara said wisely. "I'm really sorry about what happened last night."

"It wasn't all your fault." Adam stuffed his hands in his pockets and shook his head.

He chanced a tenuous smile. "Friends again?"

"Of course," she said, relieved.

"Good. I was afraid I might have to grovel."

"Would you have?" She was amused at the shy, little-boy look on his face.

"Maybe. Why? Are you planning to take back your forgiveness?"

"Nope." Sara held out the empty coffeepot. "I'll be your buddy forever, as long as you go back to making the morning coffee."

Adam grinned and took the pot from her. "Done. Now go get dressed. Please. For both our sakes."

As he watched her walk away, his smile faded. Clearly, Sara had no idea how much her continued presence was affecting him. How hard it was getting to keep from taking her in his arms and kissing her senseless.

He snorted derisively. *Senseless* was right. Nothing about his affection for her made sense. Yet he cared. Deeply. Thank heavens she didn't know how he felt.

Having Bobby Joe under foot all day Saturday, as promised, helped keep Sara's mind off Adam. It didn't totally eliminate her awareness of her handsome host but it did temper the underlying tension affecting them both.

When the boy finally went home, Sara found that her conversation skills had vanished. Nothing she tried to talk about seemed important. Not even her plans for the following day. It was going to be a long night. Probably the longest of her life.

She was pretending to read to avoid eye contact with Adam when she remarked offhand, "Did you see the pretty blouse and skirt Bobby brought? You were right about his mother's clothes fitting me."

He nodded. "Lou's probably would have, too, except that she's taller. And older."

"Right. Can I leave the clothes with you? To return, I mean?"

"Sure. The kid is probably going to drive me nuts on a regular basis, anyway. I'll send them home with him."

"Oh, dear. I hadn't thought of that. Do you want me to tell him not to bother you?"

"He's okay. If he visits too often I'll just sic the dog on him."

Sara chuckled. "Oh, sure. That'll scare him. Who wants to get licked to death? Dog kisses. Ugh!"

Disgusted with herself, she pressed her lips into a thin line. Kisses? Did you have to mention kisses? What a doofus! After what happened last night, you should know better. She grimaced. After what happened last night, she was a walking sheet of blank paper. And just about as useless. Her mind was mush. Probably *cornmeal* mush, considering how much of the stuff she'd eaten since she'd arrived. Even her thoughts didn't track!

And it was all Adam's fault. Him and his kisses. Those wonderful, tender kisses that had almost made her forget everything else.

Chapter Fifteen

Bobby arrived early Sunday morning, right on schedule. He burst in the door without knocking and made straight for the stove to help himself to a piece of bacon.

"Be my guest," Adam said sarcastically.

"Thanks." The boy looked around the room. "Miss Sara ready yet?"

"She must be. She's been in the bathroom for an hour."

Bobby giggled. "Yeah. My sisters are like that, too. You need two bathrooms, like we got."

"It's *have*," Adam said. "Like we *have*."

"Okay. Whatever." He whistled through his teeth as the door to the bathroom opened. "Wow!"

Adam didn't want to look. He knew Sara was going to be attractive in the pale-blue outfit Lou had loaned her. There wasn't a thing about his house-guest that he didn't like, anyway. In the softly flow-ing skirt and blouse, he assumed she'd be even more beautiful. If that was possible.

He gave in to the urge to peek. His eyes widened. It was possible, all right. More than possible. Sara Stone was the most stunning sight he'd ever beheld. Her long, golden hair fell in gentle waves around her face. Her skin glowed with the kiss the sun had put on her cheeks. Her eyes were clear and spar-kling.

She smiled at him. "There's still time, if you want to change your mind and go with us."

"No, thanks." Adam shook his head. He'd thought it all through, over and over again. There was no way he could attend the meeting without hearing the sermon. Without facing his disappoint-ment in God. He didn't intend to put himself through that kind of trial. It was bad enough that the nightmares about Gene had started recurring.

"Okay. Suit yourself." She turned her attention to Bobby. "Just let me put on my sandals and I'll be ready to go. Are you sure I don't need to bring food?"

"Naw. Mamaw's bringin' plenty. We always have way more than we need."

Adam handed her a light jacket. "You'd better take this. It's supposed to be warm today but you never know in the Ozarks. The weather can change in minutes.''

''Tell me about it,'' Sara said, making a silly face. ''That's how I got stuck up here in the first place.'' She draped the jacket over her shoulders. ''Thanks. Now, what about my car? Do you suppose they got it towed down the mountain okay, like they promised?''

Bobby piped up. ''If it was blue and real dirty. I saw a car and a muddy truck parked at the store when I came by.''

Well, that was that, she realized. Her mood plummeted. The last good excuse to stay near Adam Callahan was gone.

''I'll hike down there and look it over for you while you're with Bobby,'' Adam said. ''Make sure it's safe. Then, when you get back...''

''Right.'' Sara was afraid the thought of leaving him was going to make her cry. She headed for the door and hurried out onto the porch to hide her feelings.

''Take the dog with you,'' Adam called after her.

She paused but refused to look directly at him, to let him see her unshed tears. ''Why? I thought you said it was safe now.''

''I'm sure it is. I'd just feel better if Samson were along. He behaves better for you than he does for me, anyway. You shouldn't have any problems with him."

The dog never has been hard to figure out, she thought cynically. It's his master who gives me fits! "All right. Samson can go. But if he steals any food while we're in church, I'm blaming it on you."

Bobby tugged on her hand. "It's not like a real church. It's outside. That's why they call it a brush arbor."

"I know, honey." Sara managed a smile. "Remember, church isn't a building, either. It's people who believe. Like you and me."

"That's what Mamaw says."

"I'll bet it is." She stepped off the porch and started across the yard without looking back to see if Adam was watching. "I'm glad you asked me to go with you this morning, Bobby Joe. I need to get away, to get my mind focused on the things that are really important."

"Like Jesus?"

"Yes." Bobby's innocent answer to her heartfelt plea for understanding touched her, brought fresh tears to her eyes. There *were* more important things than a broken heart, weren't there? It was just so hard to remember that when her world felt as if it were falling apart around her.

Shame filled her. Compared to Adam, she'd had no problems at all. What must it have been like for him to lose his brother in such a violent, senseless way? A way that left him feeling directly responsible. No wonder he was bitter. She just wished she'd been able to show him that his healing lay in the very same faith he'd abandoned.

I'm sorry, Father. I failed you, Sara thought. There must have been something else she could have done or said. Something that would have helped Adam accept his loss and move on. If only she'd been better versed in the Word, maybe she could have quoted scripture to him.

But that wouldn't have worked if he wasn't willing to hear the truth, she realized with a start. If she'd sounded too spiritual instead of just being herself, she and Adam would probably never have become friends. And he wouldn't have felt comfortable telling her about his brother, either.

A heavy weight lifted from her soul. Peace filled her. The Lord knew what He was doing. She didn't have to see the end result to participate in Adam's ongoing healing.

But I'd like to see it, Sara added, a bit ashamed to be asking. *Please, Father. I love him. Let me know he's going to be all right.*

Adam had planned to do the breakfast dishes before going to check on Sara's car but a feeling of foreboding wouldn't let him delay. The cabin was too quiet. Too empty. Like it or not, he'd gotten used to having company. Used to Sara.

Heading for Burnham's, he'd intended to check with his friends one more time to reassure himself that Sara was in no danger. Halfway there he remembered it was Sunday. He couldn't use the phone because the store would be closed.

Muttering under his breath, Adam kept on. "She'll be all right. She'll be fine. She *has* to be."

Cresting the last ridge, he looked down on the gravel parking lot of the general store. His truck sat next to the blue hatchback Sara'd been driving. Off to one side, a tow truck was unhitching a fairly new, sport utility vehicle he didn't recognize.

Adam started down the hill as fast as he could go, sliding and slipping most of the way. He hit the bottom at a run and waved down the truck driver as he was about to leave.

"Hey, wait!"

The man leaned out the window of his rig and spat tobacco juice on the ground. "Can I help you?"

"Yes." Adam was fighting to catch his breath. He pointed. "That four-by-four. The black one. Where did it come from?"

"Up by Cheney Hill. Why? It yours?"

"No. Don't you know who it belongs to?"

"Nope. Sheriff sent me to fetch it. Figured maybe it was stolen. The folks who live out that way said it'd been parked there for over a week."

Adam's gut knotted. "What else did they say?"

The driver frowned. "Who's askin'?"

"I am." He pulled out his wallet and briefly displayed his old ID, hoping the man wouldn't look too closely and realize he had no authority. "Police."

"Well, that's different. The neighbors said some guy'd been livin' out of it, near as they could tell. Looked like it to me, too. There was cans and trash all around it when I went to get it."

"Did you see him?"

"Nope. Just the mess he left."

"How about tracks? Anything."

The driver shrugged, spat again. "Look, mister. I ain't no cop. I just drive this truck and haul cars. Okay?"

"Yeah. Sorry," Adam said. "Thanks. You can go, now."

He waited until the truck drove away, then approached the black four-wheel-drive. It wasn't locked. Hands trembling, he opened the glove compartment and reached for the registration.

It said, "Eric Rydell."

"Is it much farther?" Sara asked.

Bobby shook his head. "Nope. We'll be there in about a half hour." He grinned up at her. "I'm real proud you could come, Miss Sara. I never had a teacher I liked, before."

"I'm glad we met, too," she said. "Did you tell your grandmother about your glasses, yet?"

The boy kicked a loose rock on the trail, expertly launching the small projectile into the air. "No. I figured, well…maybe you could do that when you see her today?"

"If you want me to. You can't be expected to read if you can't see the words, you know."

"Yeah. That makes sense. You're real smart, you know that?"

Thinking of her nonexistent relationship with Adam she made a cynical face. "In some areas I may be. In others, though, I'm a real dummy."

"That's okay. Mamaw says we all have things we're good at, like God gives us gifts and stuff. She says, if we were all the same, it wouldn't be no…be any…fun."

"You're certainly right about that," Sara agreed. Pensive, sighing, she took in the natural beauty all around her. In the open areas, where sunlight reached the ground, tiny wildflowers bloomed. Some looked like miniature violets, while longer stems held cascades of delicate blue blossoms only a quarter the size of a thimble.

Overhead, swallows dipped and soared on gentle currents of air, celebrating the warm, beautiful day and feeding on insects as they flew.

"It's very beautiful here," Sara said. "I hope you realize that."

"It's okay. The fishin's real good."

She laughed. "I guess an appropriate appreciation of nature all depends on your perception."

"Guess so." Bobby looked at her quizzically. "Whatever you said." They heard Samson barking in the distance. "Sounds like the fool dog's treed another squirrel."

"Uh-oh." Sara cupped her hands around her mouth and called, "Samson…!" then waited. Nothing happened.

"He'll catch up to us," the boy said. "You can't lose a smart dog. They always find their way."

"I suppose you're right. I just don't want him showing up at the meeting and getting into the picnic food while we're all busy listening to the preacher." She shouted louder. "Samson! Samson, you get over here!"

"He pro'bly won't come while he's got his eye on the squirrel," Bobby offered. "Doesn't sound like he's very far away, though."

"Do we have time to chase after him? I don't want to be late for church."

"We won't be. I didn't know how fast you could walk in a dress, so I came to get you real, real early. You want to wait here while I go fetch him?"

"Me? Wait alone in the woods when I don't have a clue which way is home? No way." She took the boy's hand. "Just don't drag me through any brambles and tear my borrowed clothes, okay? I wouldn't want your mother to be mad at me."

"She won't be."

"Oh? How can you be sure?"

"Because that's not her outfit. Mamaw bought it for you down in Mountain Home when she found out you needed one."

"She went to all that trouble for me?"

"Sure. She's always doin' stuff like that. For poor folks and such."

"How sweet." Sara was deeply touched. Her yearly salary was probably a lot more than Bobby's family earned, yet compared to her they *were* the wealthy ones, weren't they? They gave what they could to help those in need. And in turn, the Lord had blessed them greatly.

It was an example worth remembering.

Frantic, Adam ran to the store and began pounding on the door, hoping the Burnhams hadn't already left for church. They'd have heard him if their apartment had been *three* stories above the store instead of merely one, considering the awful racket he was making. Nobody responded.

He decided against breaking a window and letting himself in so he could use the telephone to alert the sheriff. Chances were good that the small-town law officer was in church, too. Besides, what could he tell him if he did manage to reach him? No one knew where Rydell had gone after he'd abandoned the car. It was a cold trail.

The one important fact Adam did know was Sara's whereabouts for the next several hours. Finding her, warning her, was the smartest option. The question was whether it was best to take his truck and drive the long way around, or cut across through the forest on foot.

"Think. Calm down and use your head," he told himself. "You're no good to her if you go running off in the wrong direction."

His gaze focused on a slip of paper pinned to the door. Normally, he wouldn't have paid any attention to it. This note, however, had his own name scrawled at the top.

Adam ripped it down and read, "Callahan. You were right. Rydell has a record. Charged with assault. Never prosecuted. Good luck."

"No!" he shouted. "No!"

Stunned, he stared at the scrap of paper. He'd sensed from the start that it was his job, his destiny, to watch over Sara Stone. And he'd reneged on his duty. Convinced himself she'd be fine simply because he didn't want to go to the brush arbor revival with her.

Fisting the note, he raced for his truck. He'd drive home, get his gun, then set off cross-country on foot, the way she'd gone. That was his best chance of finding her before Rydell did.

The idea of Sara being in mortal danger frightened him beyond words. And it was all his fault.

There was no denying what he'd done. Or why. Sara represented the faith he'd renounced. He'd sent her away because he wasn't prepared to make his peace with God over the loss of his brother. To be involved with spiritual things might mean he'd be called upon to give up the anger he'd been nurturing for years. Anger that had been the main focus of his existence for far too long.

"I wasn't ready, before," he admitted, looking to the heavens. "But I am now. Please, God. Just take care of Sara for me till I can get there and I'll never doubt you again. I swear it."

"I think I see Samson," Bobby called over his shoulder. "Hey, he's tied to a tree!"

"He's what?" The boy had gotten way ahead of her. Sara worked her way through the underbrush, taking care to keep from snagging her skirt. Dried leaves tickled her feet through the open toes of her sandals. "How could he be tied up?"

"I don't know, but—" The boy's words were cut off in mid-sentence. Samson, too, was silent.

"Bobby? Bobby, talk to me. Where did you go?"

A man answered, "He's over here. With me."

Her heart leaped to her throat. The world spun. She staggered. Faltered. That voice! That awful voice. It couldn't be Eric. Not after all this time. But it was. Sara knew it without a doubt.

"Keep coming," he said. "That's it. Straight ahead."

Every instinct inside her screamed, *turn and run.* It was a primitive survival impulse. And for someone who didn't care what happened to others, it would have been the right thing to do. For Sara, however, it was out of the question. Eric had Bobby. And Samson. They were both helpless. She couldn't abandon them.

Steeling herself for what was to come, she followed the instructions and stepped into the clearing.

Chapter Sixteen

"Don't hurt the boy. I'm here," Sara said. The strength and composure in her voice surprised her. She straightened, standing tall.

"All dressed up, too," Eric said, dangling a pistol from his fingers. "My, my. That certainly is odd, way out here in the boondocks."

"I was on my way to church." She began to inch her way around the perimeter of the clearing. If only she could get to Bobby. Put him behind her. Shield him, somehow.

And then what do I do? Her pulse pounded in her temples. She couldn't take a deep breath. Heightened senses fed her more information than her whirling mind could effectively handle.

"Ah, yes. Church," Eric drawled. "You always were big on that kind of stuff. Too bad you quit going. We all missed you."

"I'll bet you did."

His laugh was contemptuous. "Now, now, Sara. What happened to 'turn the other cheek'?"

"I prefer the verse about the 'full armor of the Lord,'" she said. She'd reached the boy. Quickly she stepped between him and danger.

Bobby clung to her skirt and looked up at her. "Who's he? What's he want?"

"Hush," Sara said softly. Acting as a shield, she put one hand behind her and motioned for him to untie Samson.

Eric gestured with the pistol. "Forget the dog. He can't help you. Nothing can."

"What are you going to do?"

"Well, I was going to take you with me, claim what's mine, but you've complicated everything. Leave it to you to team up with a kid. You always did have a soft spot for the little brats, didn't you?"

"Bobby has nothing to do with this," Sara said. "You can let him go."

"Oh, I don't know about that. He looks pretty bright to me. And I can see he's attached to you. If I let him go, next thing I know, I'll have the law on my tail."

The press of Samson's huge body on her leg told Sara he was now beside her. Fangs bared, he faced the man and gave voice to a throaty bark.

"Shut him up or he's target practice," Eric warned.

Sara laid a steadying hand on the dog's broad head. "Good boy. It's okay. Take it easy."

"That's better," Eric said. He gestured with the gun. "Now. Come here to me."

Adam heard Samson's bark echoing across the hills. It was impossible to pinpoint the direction it came from.

"Please, God," he prayed aloud. "Which way? Which way?"

A reassurance enveloped him. Directed him. Spurred him on. He didn't know why he'd chosen as he had, he simply knew his decision was the right one. It had to be.

As he ran, parts of his mind argued against accepting any strategy he couldn't logically explain. It wasn't sensible to go charging around in the woods when he wasn't sure which path Bobby had chosen. If he wanted to find Sara before Eric did, he should have a plan. Take a rational course.

Only a rational approach took time. Adam didn't have any time to spare. Unless he chose to trust the Lord completely, there was no way he was going to succeed. No way he was going to reach Sara before Eric had a chance to harm her.

Adam's lungs ached for more air. His legs were leaden. He stumbled repeatedly. Picked himself up. Ran on. Suddenly, he felt the urge to slow down.

Gasping, he halted. Listened. Just over the next ridge, a man was speaking.

"...so you see how it is. I have no choice."

"Of course you have a choice," Sara said. "We all do. It's not enough to just sit in church on Sunday, Eric. I've tried to tell you that all along. Unless Jesus is a part of your life all the time, you'll never be truly happy."

"Hah. Like you are right now, I suppose? If your life is so perfect, how come you're here, like this?"

"I don't know." Sara's voice was calm, soothing. "Maybe because I'm not perfect. None of us are. I guess that's one of the reasons I came to the Ozarks. I was questioning my faith. Looking for my place in God's kingdom. When I..."

A flash of color over Eric's shoulder caught her eye. Samson saw it, too. The dog tensed. His ears pricked up. Before she could hide her relief, Eric read her expression and started to whirl.

Adam charged. Leaped. Hit Eric squarely and knocked him off his feet. All Sara saw was a blur of action. In seconds, Adam stood over the disarmed assailant while Samson worried the fabric of Eric's pant leg.

Bobby jumped around, applauded and cheered. "Yeah! All right!"

Suddenly weak-kneed, Sara pressed her fingers to her lips and began to weep for joy. "Oh, Adam. Am I glad to see you!"

He blinked back moisture in his own eyes. "Yeah. I know what you mean." Reaching for her, he pulled her close. "Are you all right?"

"Yes. Yes, I think so." She managed a smile. "If being scared to death doesn't count."

"Oh, it counts, honey. It definitely counts." He eyed his prisoner. "I wish I'd brought handcuffs."

"We've got *rope*," Bobby said with enthusiasm. "Can I tie him up?"

"I'll do it." Adam stuffed his pistol back in his belt and dragged Eric to his feet, slamming him against a sturdy tree. "Hands behind you."

"She's a tramp," he snarled. "I should have given up on her long ago."

"Yes, you should have," Adam countered. "But you did me a favor."

"What favor? Hey, not so tight!"

Adam didn't loosen the rope. If he'd given his emotions free rein he might have done something he'd really regret. Thank God he'd found Sara in time!

The adrenaline rush of combat still surged through him. Still prodded him to act. Finished with his task, he embraced Sara, holding her so tightly they were as one.

"Oh, Adam! I prayed you'd come," she whispered, trembling and clinging to him.

"I've been doing a lot of praying the past few minutes, too," he admitted softly.

She looked up at him, her eyes wide, wet with tears of relief. "You have?"

"Yes. And this time, the Lord heard me."

"He always does," she said tenderly. "It's the answers we get that we don't always like or understand."

"I like this one," Adam said. Bending, he placed a tender kiss on her forehead. "Do you feel like walking a little more?"

"Why?"

"We need to find a phone so we can call the sheriff and turn in our prisoner. I figure we may as well go on to church and call from one of the houses nearby."

"Church? Together?"

Adam nodded. "You bet. I'm not about to let go of you. Not for a long time. Besides, I have a debt to pay. I made the Lord a promise and I intend to keep it."

Cheering, Bobby Joe jumped high in the air. "Wahoo!"

"I think your newest student is happy," Adam said.

Sara slipped one arm around his waist as they started on the last leg of their journey. She smiled up at the man she loved with all her heart and quietly said, "He's not the only one, Callahan. I'm pretty thrilled, myself."

* * *

Sara heard the sweet gospel singing long before she saw the congregation gathered in the tranquil valley. Holding hands, she and Adam joined the assembled worshipers while Bobby ran off to find his siblings.

The scene was like a step back in time. There was an actual brush arbor, woven from saplings and the wild grape vines so prevalent in the area. The arbor wasn't large enough to cover the entire area but it did make a lovely archway in which the pastor and song leader stood.

The hymns were old, familiar friends. Stories about crossing the Jordan River, trusting in God, looking to the cross for strength. And over it all was a sense of belonging. Of homecoming.

Adam found Sara an empty folding chair in the rear and led her to it. He spoke quietly. "Wait for me here. I need to go make that call to the sheriff."

She held tight to his hand and shook her head. "No way, mister. I'm your Siamese twin from now on."

"I'll be right back. I promise." He bent lower to add, "Have I ever steered you wrong?"

"You mean other than sending me out in the rain and mud to fetch wood you didn't need? Or telling me we were having boiled owl for dinner?"

Adam's smile grew lopsided, mischievous. "Well, nobody's perfect."

"You're right about that," she countered. "Lately, though, I think you've gotten lots closer."

"You're not so bad, yourself."

"Thanks." Sara squeezed his hand. "I really don't want you to leave me. Not yet. Please?"

"Okay. We'll track down a phone, together. Come on. That house across the road looks good."

Taking his arm and gazing up at him, Sara murmured, "The house isn't the only good-looking thing I see. Tell me, when's your birthday?"

"In August. Why?"

"Because I'm going to buy you a cellular phone as a present, that's why. It's nuts to live way out in the sticks with no decent means of communication."

"I never saw a need, till now. I guess you're right."

"Glad you agree. I'll even spring for a year's service if you'll accept it as a gift."

"That's not necessary. Really."

"I don't want to put an extra burden on your finances," Sara said candidly. When Adam laughed, she added, "What? What's so funny?"

"You think I'm broke?"

"Well, maybe not broke. But you do live very frugally. I just thought…"

"I have investments that keep me more than comfortable," Adam said. "I can even afford to feed the odd stray that wanders into my life." He laid his hand over hers where it rested on his arm. "Like *you*, for instance."

By the time they returned, the last song was ending. Dressed in blue jeans and a western shirt, the preacher began to tell his congregation about the promises of God and the power of prayer.

Adam sat transfixed. Everything the man said made sense. Hadn't he just proved it for himself? Yet there was something missing. Something niggling in the back of Adam's mind that he couldn't quite put his finger on. When the call came for rededication, he suddenly knew what that something was. Raising his hand in acceptance, he came back to the God he had once denounced.

Tears of joy slid down Sara's cheeks. Her prayer had been answered. Just like the verse the pastor had quoted from the book of Jeremiah. "'Call unto me and I will answer thee and show thee great and mighty things which thou knowest not.'"

She'd called. Asked for the wisdom to help heal Adam's broken heart. And God had answered. It didn't matter that the Lord had chosen to use adversity rather than clever words from her to accomplish His divine purpose. The result was what counted.

So, her work there was done, she reasoned. The whole scheme had come to an end perfectly. And sadly, for her. She hated the idea of leaving the peace and love she'd found. Of leaving Adam. Yet what other choice did she have? Her job, her whole life, was in another place, far from the Ozarks. Far from the one man whose mere glance could send her thoughts spinning out of control, make her heart pulse with anticipation.

She'd have to go away, as planned, unless... *Unless what?* Unless she groveled? Threw herself at Adam? Begged him to let her stay? Eesh! Some choices!

The congregation stood for dismissal. Everyone started milling around, offering hospitality and making the newcomers feel welcome. Distracted, Sara shook hand after hand, glad to be in such a congenial group but wishing she and Adam could spend their last few hours alone, instead.

He finally broke away and steered her toward the long tables covered with mounded bowls and platters of food. "Come on. I didn't eat any breakfast. I'm hungry."

"I'm not."

That gave him pause. "You're not? That's a surprise. You about ate me out of house and home this past couple of weeks." He expected the gibe to make her smile, especially since she now knew he could afford it. It didn't.

Sara sighed, dreamy-eyed. "Was that all it was? It seems like I've known you forever."

"I know what you mean. I suppose that comes from living together."

"Hush! You want to get us thrown out?"

"Can't throw us out," Adam countered. "We're already outside." He spread his arms wide. "See?"

"Very funny. You know what I meant."

"Yeah, I do. Come with me. I think we need to talk more privately." He led her aside, beneath the brush arbor that now stood nearly deserted, and took both her hands. "I saw your car this morning. It looks awful. I think you should call the rental agency and tell them to come pick it up, as is."

"It's unsafe?"

"Definitely. I wouldn't drive it if I were you."

"Then, I'd still be stranded up here, wouldn't I?" Sara cocked her head, looked into his eyes for reassurance, and felt her heart leap. "With you?" It was endearing to see him actually blush.

"Well, not exactly *with* me," Adam said. "We can get you a mobile home. Have it set up at your great-grandmother's old farm, if you want, so we'd be neighbors. Then I could help you fix up the place. Make it livable."

"Sounds to me like you've given this a lot of thought."

"Enough."

"And then what?"

"That's up to you." Hopeful, Adam studied her guileless expression. "I thought we could start all over. As they say in the back country, I'd come courting. Do things right.''

A grin so wide it made her cheeks hurt spread across Sara's face. ''You mean, ask me to marry you?'' she ventured.

''Well...well, sure. Eventually. After you've had a chance to get to know me better. To feel the same way about me that I feel about you.''

Her laugh was exuberant, her face radiant. ''Oh, big mistake, Callahan. Big mistake. It's way too late for that. I'm already so goofy about you I can hardly see straight.''

''You are?''

''Uh-huh. Surprised?''

''A little.'' He gathered her in his arms, oblivious to the smiles of the onlookers who had gathered around the arbor at Bobby Joe's urging. ''I suppose you're going to hold me to the part about getting married.''

''I sure am. Where and when?''

''You're the bride. That's up to you.''

Filled with so much happiness she felt as if she'd burst, Sara looked up at the arching branches above them and knew at once what her decision should be. ''I want to be married right here,'' she said. ''In the brush arbor.''

''You could have a big church wedding if you want,'' Adam offered. ''I don't mind.''

''Everything I ever wanted I found right here,''

Sara told him. "Starting with you. There's no need to go anywhere else. To search for anything else."

"I love you," Adam whispered.

"I love you, too." Tilting her face up, she wrapped her arms around his neck and urged him to kiss her.

Adam didn't need much convincing. He claimed her mouth with tenderness and a total love, made even more wonderful by the peace that now nurtured his soul.

In the background, Bobby Joe cheered and his extended family applauded loudly.

Sara giggled. "I think we're going to have a pretty big guest list. Are you sure you don't mind?"

"As long as they don't try to come on our honeymoon with us," Adam said, "I have no objections at all."

She slipped her arm around his waist and stood beside him, facing their new friends and grinning foolishly. "I'll need a couple of months to prepare," she said. "How does a fall wedding sound?"

"Fine." Adam tried not to let his disappointment show. He'd live through the long wait somehow. "I understand how you'd want to go back home to Chicago and pack your things. But will it take you that long to move?"

"No, not at all," Sara said, eager to deliver the punch line and put Adam's mind at ease. "I'll just need some extra time beyond that."

"What for?"

She grinned up at him, her eyes twinkling, her heart overflowing with love, with the joy of living, and said, "Why, to train Samson to be my flower dog, of course."

Epilogue

The planned September wedding was scheduled to take place in late August, instead, because the preacher had an opening in his calendar. At least that was the excuse Sara gave. In truth, she wanted to belong to Adam completely and wasn't willing to tempt her guardian angels any further.

Instead of an electric organ for music, some of the wedding guests brought guitars. A quartet sang as Sara walked down the aisle.

Dressed in a dark suit and looking more handsome than ever, Adam was waiting for her beneath the same brush arbor. Samson sat at his feet. Bobby Joe's sisters had decorated both the arch and the dog's collar with flowers. The sky was bright, the breeze just enough of the breath of God to cool the late-summer air and make the day perfect.

Sara's heart swelled at the sight of her beloved, at his expression of eagerness. She cherished him so. The tenderhearted man he'd been trying to hide when she'd first met him was now in control. The prankster who'd teased her so unmercifully was still around, too, much to her delight.

She glided down the aisle on Bobby Joe's arm. The perfect bride with the perfect escort. Her gown was a simple, unadorned sheath, her bouquet the wildflowers currently in bloom in the hills. The same flowers decorated her hair.

Adam took her hand, smiled down at her, and the ceremony began. Sara was so breathless with excitement she was afraid she'd faint if Adam dared let go.

Then, almost before it had begun, it was over. They were husband and wife. One in the Lord. Together forever.

*   *   *   *   *

Dear Reader,

Each of us is blessed with special talents. Writing happy, uplifting love stories like this one is simply one of them. I believe as long as we make the most of God's gifts to us, whatever they may be, we can't help but find a measure of peace and satisfaction.

When some of my prayer partners seem awed because I'm a published author, I remind them that they, too, are vitally important to the Lord. So, dear reader, are you.

We can all be parts of a greater plan, a greater good. The possibilities are endless. If you have never given God control of your life, I urge you to do it right now and find out how miraculous ordinary, daily life can be. I did—and I've never been sorry.

For me, there was no special formula, no perfect prayer necessary for success. The scripture I chose as the theme of this book is *Jeremiah* 33:3, "Call unto me and I will answer you and will tell you great and hidden things which you have not known." And in *James* 4:2, it says, "You have not because you ask not."

The characters in this story found out how true those verses are. I pray that you will, too. I'd love to hear from you at P.O. Box 13, Glencoe, AR 72539-0013.

Valerie Hansen